MOONBIRD

MOONBIRD

GRANIA DAVIS

DOUBLEDAY & COMPANY, INC.
GARDEN CITY, NEW YORK
1986

All of the characters in this book are fictitious, and any resemblance to actual persons, living or dead, is purely coincidental.

Library of Congress Cataloging-in-Publication Data

Davis, Grania.
Moonbird.
I. Title.
PS3554.A93456M6   1986   813'.54   85-16077
ISBN: 0-385-19555-9
Copyright © 1986 by Grania Davis
All Rights Reserved
Printed in the United States

First Edition

For Philip K. Dick
—Who flew like a butterfly to join the others on the far shore . . .

According to Balinese tales, each person has both godlike and demonic traits. When these traits lose their harmonious balance, disease and chaos appear . . .

MOONBIRD

I

A god came to Madai when he was just a young boy . . .

1

The shadow puppets danced in the ghostly light of the flickering oil lamps, and the children huddled together in the steamy night, watching with wide obsidian eyes. They had seen the ancient battle of gods and demons many times, but the swirl of music and movement lured them with unearthly dreams.

The *dalang*, master of the puppets, had already entered a deep trance. He sat alone behind a translucent screen and manipulated his mythical troupe. They mimed and capered as he chanted in the voice of one character, then another, while the *gamelan* musicians wove their intricate rhythms.

Are the puppets aware of their master, Madai wondered? *Or do they believe they control their own fates?*

Twelve-year-old Madai shifted on his straw mat in the temple courtyard, and snuggled against his older sister, Dawan. Sputtering torches illuminated the clearing. Beyond was the dark equatorial forest of sprawling banyans and bamboos. Sea winds carried spatters of warm rain, and the scent of clove and curry over the crowd that sprawled before the stage—on this small island near Bali.

The villagers had trekked to this remote sandstone and thatch temple to enjoy the full moon festival that would last all night. Vendors set up little stands at the edge of the clearing to sell betel and sweet coconut cakes, clove-scented kretek cigarettes and palm wine, Java coffee and Bintang beer, grilled, skewered pork with tamarind and peanut sauce, and peppery fried noodles with sliced onions and shrimp.

Young couples in colorful batik sarongs gently teased and flirted in the shadows of the mossy temple walls. Infants and grannies dozed contentedly on the mats as scrawny dogs, chickens, and pigs nosed for scraps.

The puppets were lacy silhouettes of leather worked with beaten silver. They moved in an elaborate choreography behind their kerosene-lit screen. A magical Barong dragon, with a massive lion's head and mane, swayed with deliberate grace to the bubbling gamelan melody. The Barong stopped and listened intently. A prince and his servant were traveling at night through the haunted forest, talking fearfully of *leyak* spirits. Meanwhile a leyak wearing a cloth of invisibility over his head tiptoed closely behind them and listened to every word.

The children giggled nervously at the antics of the leyak. It was amusing on the puppet stage, but Madai wouldn't want an invisible leyak following *him* through the forest shadows.

Barong tried to warn the startled men, and the leyak slipped away. They all traveled together until they came upon the small wicker hut of Rangda, the evil sorceress.

The crowd grew tense and the drums and gongs pounded wildly. Nobody on the island laughed at Rangda, the source of all misfortune. Rangda was the mother of an ancient Balinese King. Because she practiced black magic, she was exiled into the forest. She took revenge by cursing the people—and she curses their descendants to this day.

Rangda appeared at the door of her hut, and whipped a cloth of invisibility from her head. The dalang worked the puppet sticks so the prince and his servant cried out and shivered with terror. The horrible face of Rangda appeared before them with bulging eyes, sharp fangs, and tangled hair. Her long claws trembled.

Barong leaped into action, chasing the witch across the puppet stage with snapping jaws. The leyak reappeared to aid the witch, and the men drew their powerful *kris* daggers. The gongs and drums clashed with excitement as Barong and the men fought the sorceress and her ally.

Madai gripped the hand of his favorite cousin, Lasmi.

The battle surged wildly back and forth across the translucent screen while the entranced puppet master uttered inarticulate grunts and cries.

The prince raised his glittering kris and tried to stab Rangda with the wavy blade. She stared at him with malevolent eyes and he collapsed. The servant and the leyak struggled furiously as Barong and Rangda reeled across the screen. With a sudden strike, the dragon-protector lunged at the witch and shoved her offstage. The leyak followed, and they both disappeared. Barong revived the prince with his breath, and they all continued their journey through the dark, haunted forest.

"*The play is ended, but the story goes on forever* . . ." chanted the entranced puppet master. Then his voice trailed into silence.

"Why didn't Barong kill Rangda?" asked Madai's little brother, Ketut.

"*Beh!*" cried their older sister, Dawan. "You mustn't say that. If Rangda were killed in the shadow play, her spirit would grow angry. She would curse the puppet master and he'd fall ill and die. And if the spirit of Rangda hears you say such things—she'll curse *you!*"

The small boy whimpered and buried his face in his sister's lap.

2

Madai pulled a conical straw basket from a bamboo rafter, and slung the hemp strap across his skinny brown shoulder.

"Going to catch blue crabs in the river?" asked his mother, sitting on the verandah straining coco-milk. A colorful batik sarong was tucked loosely around her waist and she wore an amulet of rough-cut moonstones around her neck.

"Going into the forest to pick passion fruit," said Madai.

"Good. They're sweet and juicy now." His mother's broad-cheeked smile revealed several missing teeth. "But stay far from the graveyard. There are leyak spirits about. My cousin saw strange-looking lights last night, and her neighbor saw a pig running—with a white monkey and a rooster perched on its back."

"Sure, Ibu," said Madai casually. His mother was so superstitious. Madai was now fourteen years old, and had attended four years of mission school. He could *read*. He had learned that the tiny green vipers and scorpions that scuttle in the forest debris are much more dangerous than the vague leyak spirits.

Father Hans and the mission teachers were superstitious too, with their murdered god who multiplied loaves and fishes. Madai lived near a river and the sea. He knew that if you want fish, you catch them—one by one.

"Come on, Madai!" called his friends below. "Don't make us stand here in the beating sun."

Madai tucked his short sarong tightly around his waist, and raced down the creaking bamboo ladder of his mother's rattan and palm-thatch cookhouse. The group of slight, dark-eyed children waited for him in the filigreed shade of the loosely woven wicker walls of his family compound.

The little band scampered between rows of leafy mango trees that lined the muddy village pathway into the forest. The powerful mid-morning equatorial sun beat down upon the children, and deepened the colors of the foliage that lavishly blanketed their island.

Madai's second cousin, Lasmi, cheerfully linked her tawny arm through his. She was a tall, sturdy girl of twelve, with long, thick black hair.

The pathway cut across the grassy meadow that bordered the communal *desa* village of wicker compounds, and rattan houses with peaked palm-thatch roofs, built upon low platforms supported by thick bamboo stilts.

At the edge of the clearing, before the pathway snaked into the deep green shadows of the forest, they paused before a tall arched gateway of mossy, elaborately carved sandstone.

This was the entrance to the village temple. Carved into the weathered stones were the creatures of the old god-tales that had been brought to the islands by Hindu traders long centuries ago.

Brama the Creator, Siva the Destroyer, Visnu the Preserver, Garuda the Eagle God, the Nagas, who are the dragons of the sea, and the monstrous face of Rangda the witch. They were as familiar to the children as the faces of the villagers.

The mission priest gently insisted that *his* god-tales were better. Maybe so. The amiable villagers were willing to include the crucified image in a small side shrine. Father Hans wanted *only* his god upon the altar. That made the villagers laugh. How could they rely upon a god who couldn't even protect himself from murderers?

"Listen, they're chanting puja," said Lasmi.

From the heavily thatched, seven-tiered pagoda, which was the main temple building, Madai heard the chanting of the Brahman priests, and the melodious reed instruments, gamelans, and gongs that accompany the puja.

"It's the full-moon ceremony to placate Rangda," said Lasmi, her black eyes shining with excitement. "Let's watch."

"Rangda scares me," whimpered Madai's little brother, Ketut.

"Then you must chant the puja for protection," said Lasmi in her bossy tone.

Ketut fidgeted uneasily and pulled at her hand. He was trapped by Lasmi, his older attendant—and knew it.

The children entered the ornate temple gateway. Inside the compound two smaller, three-tiered pagodas flanked the main building, whose seven levels represented the seven stages of spiritual attainment, and the seven levels of the mountain in the center of the universe where the spirits of ancestors dwell.

The temples were made of lavishly carved wooden beams supporting heavy layers of dark thatch. Massive stone images of protectors and demons guarded the crumbling sandstone entrances. Meeting pavilions and lichen-covered shrines dotted the clearing.

A small crowd had gathered at the entrance of the central pagoda. Their brightest sarongs were tied around their waists, moonstone and silver amulets looped around their necks, and sweet scented frangipani flowers twined in their black hair.

The small boy whined, for despite their finery these people were not a pretty sight. They were the unfortunates of the island, gathered to hear the puja to Rangda the witch—who had cursed them.

A gnarled old man who was cursed with arthritis . . . A mother carrying a blank-eyed child cursed with idiocy . . . Scarred faces cursed with pox . . . Swollen bellies cursed with tumors . . . A leper whose cursed limbs were shriveled to dark stumps . . . Bamboo litters for those cursed with weakness . . . Youngsters cursed with runny sores that wouldn't heal, and broken bones that wouldn't mend . . . Toddlers cursed with worms and diarrhea . . . An old woman cursed with senility . . . Scarred people cursed by fire . . . A feverish woman cursed with malaria . . . A man cursed by a festering scorpion bite . . . A cursed boy born with twisted arms and legs . . . A blind woman cursed with cataracts . . . Infants cursed with sore ears . . . A thin man cursed with coughs . . . Children cursed with lice and itchy rashes . . . A pretty girl cursed with epilepsy . . .

Ketut refused to go any closer, even though bossy Lasmi prodded him. This time Madai agreed with the lad—it was near enough to view the puja. Any closer would be foolhardy.

The mission teachers said that all the sickness on the island was caused by poor sanitation, lack of modern medicine, and inbreeding. Maybe so. The mission teachers seemed to know about such practical matters. They helped the villagers fill out the census and tax forms that came each year from the remote central government on the swarming main island of Java.

Madai suspected that the central government and the vast capital were superstitions too. For few islanders had actually seen them.

The villagers had different ideas about the cause of illness. They believed it was the curse of Rangda, servant of Siva the Destroyer. That's why the sick and maimed gathered at the temple for the monthly puja to Rangda. To placate the Antagonist, and to persuade her to lift her vile spell from the supplicating and suffering faithful.

The puja was an elaborate event that lasted all day and night. First came rites of purification, when the white-robed Brahman priests blessed the crowd with silver ladles of holy water and specially blessed rice scattered in all the eleven directions, above, below, and around the earth.

Now the main part of the ceremony was unfolding. A melodious dance drama performed by the village dancers and musicians, clad in shimmering brocade sarongs and elaborate gilt and floral headdresses.

Madai and his friends uneasily watched the ancient tale of the island in a golden age free of all sickness, natural catastrophe, and death—until the arrival of the monstrous sorceress Rangda, who had been exiled from Bali with a band of rebel Brahmans.

At first the primitive forest people of the island had welcomed the new gods and their priests, and the Raja offered to marry Rangda's beautiful daughter. A Garuda-eagle warned the Raja that Rangda was a witch, and the Raja rejected her daughter. Rangda grew angry and cursed the island with a horrible pox. The islanders tried to placate the Antagonist, but her rage couldn't be appeased. She continued to spread sickness, death, and disasters—and she continues to this day.

The dancers enacted the familiar tale with graceful hand gestures, expressive faces, floating limbs and chants. Two skilled dancers appeared under the swaying body of Barong, the lion-headed dragon who protects the island. Covered with gilded leather, flowers and feathers, and flecks of glittering mica and mirrors, Barong lunged at the curtained hut where Rangda and her daughter were hiding. He shook his massive red and gold mane, so that hundreds of tiny bells tinkled.

Now the dance reached its climax. A newborn water buffalo calf bedecked with scented tampaka flowers, beaten silver, and moonstones was dragged squealing to a bamboo platform before the altar to Rangda. The shaven-headed priest sprinkled its thrashing body with holy water and rice while the dancers chanted hypnotically.

Just as the sunlight reached the full intensity of an equatorial noon, the priest slit the throat of the bleating calf as a sacrifice to the witch. The blood gushed freely, and the cursed ones pushed forward to smear their faces and limbs with fresh blood. For they were also sacrificial victims, who should be forgiven—and healed.

The chanting and music continued with measured frenzy, while skinny scavenger dogs licked their chops hungrily.

Why must some creatures eat and others be eaten, Madai wondered?

The priest drew back the curtain of the little rattan hut that hid the image of Rangda. The people wept with terror and veneration as the glistening white face came into view, with its protruding eyes and great tusks.

A tangle of coppery goat's hair hung from Rangda's head to the ground, and she wore a garland of human entrails around her neck. Flames rose behind her back to meet the tall palm banners and brocade umbrella that shaded her head. A white cloth with the magic symbols of power and invisibility was tied around her waist. Her arms and legs were covered with coarse hair, and her fingers were adorned with long, terrible nails.

The worshipers chanted wildly, and threw red hibiscus flowers at the malevolent white face that gazed at them cooly amidst the thicket of copper hair.

Perhaps it was a trick of the sunlight, but the huge cold eyes of Rangda seemed to shift and survey the imploring crowd, and the frightened, staring children. The great tusked mouth seemed to smile slightly. The tangled mass of hair seemed to sway, and the long transparent nails trembled—even though there was no breeze.

"*Beh!*" whimpered Ketut, wriggling with fear.

He bolted outside the temple gates, and the squealing band of children followed.

Madai glanced back before he ran to join the others. Rangda's wrathful eyes seemed to stare directly at him.

3

"It's just a superstition, you know," Madai explained to Lasmi as they continued into the forest. "Witches don't really cause disease."

"How can you be sure?"

"I read about it in books at the mission school. I'll show you the pictures. People get sick when teeny bugs called germs get inside their bodies, so small that you can only see them with a machine."

"If nobody can see them, how do you know the tiny bugs aren't a superstition?" asked Lasmi in her direct and sensible way. "And even if they're real, who decides where to send them? Why do they attack some people and not others? Maybe the bugs are servants of Rangda."

"Stop saying that name—you'll call her!" cried Ketut.

Madai couldn't think of a good reply. Were the tiny bugs in the mission books real, and who decides where to send them? Lasmi's questions were tough.

The children walked in the steamy afternoon heat, through groves of banyan trees whose extended network of aerial roots and branches covered acres of forest. They crossed thickets of tall, swaying bamboo used for building and every domestic purpose.

Individual rays of shimmering sunlight penetrated the gaps in the jungle, illuminating myriad shades of green. Tiny animals darted and rustled in the underbrush, and flocks of primary colored parrots swooped and screamed overhead. The children walked carefully, alert for the hiss and scuttle of small, deadly vipers.

The pathway gradually descended to a marshy area where the ground was spongy underfoot. Here the thickets were laced with a tangle of passion vines, gaily bedecked with large fragrant flowers of richly veined purple, and bright golden fruit.

The children ran to break them open, eagerly filling their mouths with the tangy pulp and crunchy black seeds. They cheerfully ate their fill as passion-fruit juice dripped down their chins. Then they fanned out among the vines to fill their conical baskets.

Madai wandered by himself to an overgrown copse that always

bore large, sweet fruit. He reached for the ripest globes, and tossed them into his basket to bring home. He hummed a little song, and enjoyed the heavy odors of the forest. He brushed sweat and gnats from his forehead. His mind was floating.

Suddenly he felt a sharp stab at his big toe—was it a green viper? No, it wasn't that painful. Probably just a rock protruding from the sticky soil. He looked down and saw something glimmering in the mud.

He bent to pick it up, and was delighted to find a small, rough-carved moonstone image of the eagle god, Garuda.

He wiped the mud off the image with his sarong, and held the tiny bird up to a sunbeam to enjoy the iridescent moonlight that glimmered inside the stone. Who had carved this creature and left it in the forest? In the shimmering light, the eyes of the bird seemed to flicker slightly.

Madai felt a dark wave of dizziness. He sat down abruptly on the soft ground and rested his head in his hands. Too much sun perhaps? He felt a movement in his hand, and glanced at the strange carving—had it grown larger?

Another wave of dizziness, then he felt something soft and smooth stroking his cheek. Was it Lasmi's hand? No, it was too cool. It had the cool smoothness of—*moonstone.*

Madai opened his eyes and saw a great, shining Garuda perched on the forest floor beside him, stroking his cheek with an iridescent wingtip.

"That's not possible," said Madai flatly.

In his mind came a whisper like the rustling of the breeze. "Most things are possible," said the Garuda.

"Are you a leyak-spirit?"

"I am the Moonbird."

"What do you want?"

"You wakened me with sunlight," whispered the bird. "What do *you* want?"

Madai and the glowing Moonbird eyed each other. Madai felt the uneasy sensation of someone trying to waken from a deep sleep. A big Garuda stood before him with bright eyes, sharply curved beak, long, graceful tail and wing feathers glimmering with the light of moonstones—whispering into his mind.

Impossible.

Yet there it was. He could see, hear, and touch it; he wasn't sick or crazed. His mother was right, she'd always warned about spirits in the forest, and now he'd seen one for himself. Like the tiny bugs that cause disease, this superstition was *real.*

He felt a silly giddiness, as though he'd drunk too much beer. Garudas are protectors, servants of Visnu the Preserver. They nest on the mountain in the center of the universe, and they aren't harmful, so no need to be afraid. But what can a fourteen-year-old boy do with a Moonbird?

"Can you fly?" Madai asked mischievously.

"Birds generally fly," whispered the Moonbird.

"Could you fly with *me* on your back?"

"If you are light enough, I can carry you," said the Moonbird.

Small, wiry Madai was sure he'd be light enough. So he climbed onto the silken back and clasped his thin brown arms around the soft, shimmering down of the Garuda's long neck.

"Fly me around the island!" he shouted.

The bird tensed its powerful muscles, and with a rustling sound lifted above the groves of banyan and bamboo. Madai was startled and frightened—he was floating above the treetops and it was scary! Could he trust the bird spirit not to drop him? He grasped the Garuda's soft neck more tightly.

The Moonbird swooped and soared above the green of the jungle, and Madai began to relax and enjoy the ride. Wait until he told Lasmi; she'd be so jealous. Better not to tell his mother though; she'd worry and forbid it.

The Moonbird flew along the broad curves of the muddy green Waringan River, which flows from the mountains that dominate the center of the island. He flew up into the foothills, pale green with terraced rice paddies. The strong afternoon sun beat down upon Madai's unprotected face and shoulders as they sailed between the deep blue of the sky and the deep green of the hillside pine forests.

They flew into the cool gray mists that perpetually swirl among the peaks, and Madai shivered as a chilly drizzle began to fall on his back. With wings outstretched to ride the wind currents, the wondrous bird flew up into the summits. Madai saw that their destination was Mount Alāka, the island's tallest peak and only active volcano. Still they flew up, up . . .

Soon the crater of Mount Alāka appeared below them, an irregular black scar above the dense mountain forest, with a steaming caldera in the center. The Moonbird landed with a rustle of wings at the desolate shore of the bubbling lake.

Madai leaped off the Moonbird to explore, but this place made him uneasy. The lake was boiling hot and smelled like rotten eggs. The folded and tumbled black lava scratched at his bare feet. What if the strange bird spirit flew away and abandoned him here? What if this were some leyak trick? Better not to stray too far.

Before he returned to the bird, he stooped to pick a single red-veined orchid that grew from the lava. It was a type unknown in his lowland village. He would keep the mountain orchid to prove to himself that this was—*real.*

Panting and shivering in the thin, drizzly mountain air, he climbed onto the gleaming back of the Moonbird. Too bad this wasn't an ordinary bird whose flesh and feathers would feel cozy and warm. But no ordinary bird would whisper into his mind and carry him through the air. He nestled his cheek against the cool moonstone feathers.

The mist darkened and the drizzle became a cold rain. Flicks of lightning glimmered and rumbled among the thick cloud banks that raced in the mountain winds.

Madai felt lonely. Had anyone ever been to the top of Mount Alāka before? Had anyone ever seen the boiling, stinking yellow lake, felt the sharp lava underfoot and the thin mountain winds? Sometimes tourists and their guides came trekking up here, laden with climbing gear and cameras. But never a solitary boy riding an unpredictable spirit.

"Fly down!" he said to the Moonbird.

Another rustle and lifting of wings; soaring and gliding on the mountain winds. Down from the desolate peaks and craggy pine forests. Down into the sunshine of the rice-terraced foothills. Down over the muddy river lined with coco-palms and tiny thatched desa villages. How small the houses look from above!

Riding the warm air currents into the welcome sunshine . . . Down, down to a powdery beach that sparkled with fragments of mica and moonstone. Down to the shoreline of the creamy blue sea.

Some islanders are afraid of the Naga dragons who live in the depths of the ocean, but this landscape held no fear for Madai. He sprang off the Moonbird, and scampered and frolicked in the frothy waves. He dived and capered in the warm water like any brave island boy who is as much at home in the sea as on the shore. He watched brightly colored schools of darting fish, resplendent in fluorescent stripes of yellow, blue, and purple.

It was several hours journey by foot or dugout, traveling along the river from his village to the sea. How grand to fly here in an instant. Then he noticed the fireball of the late afternoon sun and lavender tones in the clouds.

He scooped up a pearly, swirled sea-snail shell. Then he raced, sunburned and tired, back to the Moonbird, who stood on the beach among bowing coco-palms, as still and impassive as a stone carving. Its crystalline feathers had a ruddy tint in the sunset, and Madai wondered if the creature could still move at all. Had it solidified into a stone image, leaving Madai stranded at the beach with many kilometers to trudge home?

But again the tensed muscles and rustling wings; again the excitement of swooping and soaring on the air currents; again the giddy sensation of flying over the treetops, toy villages, and darkening river. With a little thud they landed in the familiar grove of passion vines.

Madai climbed off the Moonbird. He felt a dizzy wave and sank back down upon the spongy ground.

"Madai, *Madai!*" Someone was shaking him and calling his name. He opened one eye warily—more spirits?

It was Lasmi, looking worried and stern. "Wake up, Madai!" she cried. "Why are you sitting here in the forest sound asleep? I couldn't wake you and you kept mumbling to yourself. Aren't you afraid of vipers? So lazy, sleeping away the afternoon. And look, you hardly picked any fruit, your basket is still half empty."

Madai slowly recovered. He enjoyed the comforting normality of Lasmi's bossy chatter. He might have assumed that she was right, that he had grown drowsy in the forest warmth, and fallen asleep and dreamed it all.

Except that in his hands were a wilted red mountain orchid, a spiral seashell, and a small, rough-carved image of a moonstone Garuda.

4

"You're a strange boy, Madai," said his mother one stormy evening. The family sat by the yellow light of a kerosene lamp, listening to the rain drumming on the thatch, and eating fish and rice stewed in coco-milk. Curry spices scented the steamy air.

"You're almost sixteen now," his mother continued. "You're not tall and you've never been very strong, but your muscles are starting to fill in. Most boys your age are out on the fishing boats, or cutting wood with the men to earn their keep. But you still wander in the forest, or listen to the god-tales and the mission teachers like a child."

Madai flushed angrily. He was at an age when he didn't like anyone calling him a child—and he had his own mysterious reasons for his solitary visits to the forests.

The mission teachers were easier to explain. "I like the mission school, Ibu," said Madai. "Maybe I can get a high school diploma one day. They have science books and magazines that tell about *real* facts happening all over the world. Did you know that some years ago the Americans sent a rocket, with men to walk on the moon?"

"Did the Americans find any fish or firewood on the moon?" asked his father.

Madai's brother and sister laughed.

"But that's important, Bapak. Men walking on the moon!"

"Fish are important. Firewood, rice, and fruit are important, and with your big appetite you should spend more time gathering them, instead of mooning over books and dreaming in the forest," grumbled his father, a plump, swarthy man whose leathery face spoke of many years of direct sunlight.

"Why don't you go out on the boat with Bapak tomorrow?" asked his mother.

"Yeah, Son, it's time you learn to fish. You'll be father of a hungry family yourself one day, and you can't feed them a diploma. Come on. We have a good time out in the boats. Tell stories and jokes, drink a little Australian beer, talk about the women. You might learn something from us."

"You want me to come—tomorrow?" asked Madai, flushing again.

"Yes. What's the matter with that, you got an appointment with the Prime Minister?"

His mother and the other children laughed again. Their father was known for his good-natured wit.

"I promised to return a book to Father Hans tomorrow. It's a science book about different animals and plants."

"I'll show you animals and plants—ones you can eat!"

Actually Madai had lied. The mission priest didn't care when he returned the book. He was lying more and more now, to cover up the times he spent with the Moonbird.

Since that first day in the forest two long years ago, Madai had sought more and more solace with the Moonbird. He often went to the secret grove, and held the small moonstone carving up to the sunlight until he felt the familiar wave of dizziness. Then Moonbird would appear to take him to wondrous places and show him magical things . . . So Madai had passed two dreamlike years, as his body matured and the mangoes twice ripened and fell.

"Madai, Madai!" His mother was shouting at him, her high-cheeked face concerned. "Pay attention when I talk to you. I don't like you staring off into space like that."

"Sorry, Ibu, I was thinking."

"Thinking," snorted their father. "Try fishing for a change."

His younger brother, Ketut, and older sister, Dawan, giggled, enjoying the show.

"I'm always worried about you," said his mother. "You were so sickly and weak when you were little, and you almost died of the fevers. I prayed to Lord Visnu and he restored your health, but now you act so strange. I'm not the only one in our desa village who has noticed. Your aunt Karmi went into the forest to pick passion fruit, and saw you dreaming and mumbling like a temple dancer in a trance."

"I fell asleep."

"Sleeping in the forest? What if vipers bite you?"

"What if I go fishing with Bapak and Naga dragons drown me?"

"*Beh!* You've enjoyed the water since you were a sprout," snorted his father. "It's settled. You'll come out on the boat tomorrow."

Madai had no intention of going out on the fishing boat. He wouldn't spend his days in a cramped sailing dugout, listening to the gossip and coarse jokes of the village men.

He tossed restlessly on his mat all through the night wondering what to do, then just before dawn an idea came to him. If the Moonbird could take him anywhere, why not fly beneath the water of the reef? There he could collect conchs and lobsters to bring home.

That would satisfy his family. He knew they didn't mean to be cruel, but they had many mouths to feed and he was nearly a man now. He was expected to provide his share by gathering food for himself. Children could pick fruit in the forest, women could tend the rice paddies and vegetable gardens—but a man was expected to bring home fish.

He would bring home succulent shellfish from the bottom of the sea, and his parents would be delighted. He would try the solitary and perilous occupation of reef diving, which most men avoid from fear of mythical Nagas and poisonous rockfish. They'd all praise him. He could stay away all day, and his mother would beam as she fried the conchs and lobsters in coco-oil. His mouth began to water and the idea seemed more and more appealing.

Madai rose off his straw sleeping mat before dawn. The rain had stopped and the air was mild and humid, filled with buzzing insects and the sweet scent of creamy frangipani flowers. The sky was still dark and overcast, and a brisk breeze ruffled the coco-palms. Roosters began to crow.

Madai carried a small flashlight and a pocketknife, which the mission nuns had awarded him for top scores. He walked purposefully along the pathway toward the forest, a path so familiar that he could have walked it without any light.

He would enter the bush before any of the villagers in their close-knit desa rose for the day, summon the Moonbird, and ask to go under the sea for reef fishing. Then he'd have all day to frolic on the beach or go to the mission school, read and play until evening time, when he'd return home feigning exhaustion and laden with shellfish.

Had some biblical Moonbird been responsible for the strange miracle of multiplying fishes? Madai had never believed that missionary story before, but now he was trying a similar trick.

Could the Moonbird carry him under the water? He was sure the eagle god could do anything. Madai laughed to himself, imagining the Moonbird's typically laconic reply.

The big Garuda would say, "Birds who live near the sea are generally adept at fishing."

What a fine idea! He could already taste the shellfish that his mother would proudly fry with plantains tonight. His father would slap him on the back and give him a bottle of Bintang beer. His little brother and his diminutive older sister, Dawan, would gaze at him proudly—as a man.

Madai had already reached the carved sandstone temple gates at the edge of the jungle. Pale violet on the eastern horizon marked the beginning of sunrise on an overcast day.

He was about to enter the forest when he heard a rustling hiss in the magenta-flowered bougainvillea vines that trailed lavishly over the crumbling temple gate. Was it a viper? Curious, Madai flicked on his flashlight and trained it at the hedge.

There was a flickering shadow and a brief flash of fanged white face, long trembling nails, and tangled copper hair. Icy eyes glared at him. Was it—*Rangda!*

A large white ape with an oddly clipped tail dashed across the treetops, jabbering shrilly with alarm. Madai looked up, startled, and the apparition in the flowering vines disappeared with a sighing hiss.

Puzzled, Madai searched through the bougainvillea with his flashlight, but he could find nothing. Perhaps the shadowy light was playing tricks. He continued into the bush, feeling carefully with his bare feet and listening tensely for vipers. The dense greenery closed in around him, and the dawn birds began to hoot and call. Tiny creatures skittered through the underbrush, and mosquitoes buzzed in Madai's ears. The path sloped down through banyan groves and thickets of tall bamboo, to the marshy spot that he favored. He could hear frogs clamoring with predawn fervor. The early morning forest vibrated with life as Madai hurried to his grassy rendezvous with the Moonbird, whom he summoned with the beam of his flashlight.

"Can you carry me beneath the sea?" he asked when the shimmering Garuda appeared.

"Shorebirds are generally adept at diving," said the Moonbird.

"Let's go!" he laughed, climbing onto the Garuda's luminous back. Though he'd grown in the two strange years since he'd found Moonbird, the big Garuda still found him light enough to carry.

The tension in the sinewy muscles . . . The rustle of wings . . . The rush of excitement as they flew over the treetops and the miniature thatched desa. Then a surge of delight as they dived—without any need for breath, into the frothy blue warmth of the equatorial sea.

Down, down among the wonders of the coral reefs that ring the island.

5

They swam with suspended breath among undersea gardens of rosy coral, among schools of tiger-striped round fish, fluorescent blue fish, and small fish of sparkling silver. They swam through overgrown meadows of kelp, where the spiny, poisonous rockfish lurk, and among schools of translucent jellyfish, hovering like ghostly blobs above the fluttering pink anemone blossoms. They swam between dead coral boulders, where ruddy octopuses coiled and fat red eels twined, and past sunken boats crusted with barnacles, where tiny, transparent shrimp floated. In undersea canyons they would fill Madai's wicker basket with the succulent shellfish that his family loved.

Then a curious creature came swimming alongside them. It was a large turtle of mottled brown and green, with webs between its limbs that formed long, graceful wings.

"Greetings, Bedawang," said the Moonbird.

The winged turtle solemnly bowed its head, then spoke in a voice that burbled like water. "Basudara, the old King of the Naga dragons, has died, and the cremation ceremony will be held today. Will you come?"

"Would you like to see Bogavati, the gilded city of the Naga kings?" The Moonbird whispered to Madai.

"What about my shellfish?"

"They'll wait here until we return; they're in no hurry to be trapped inside your basket."

Madai wasn't sure. He'd been very excited about his bold plan to become a reef diver. That was *real*. Winged turtles and Naga kings were legends—so were Garudas who could carry lads under the sea without breath. It was confusing. Still, his curiosity was roused. He'd always wanted to see strange lands, and what could be stranger than the Naga kingdom?

The Moonbird followed Bedawang the Winged Turtle through a narrow cleft between twisted coral fans. Then suddenly they were falling . . . falling in the silent dark into deeper dark, like a frightening dream.

There were mists, then the golden pagodas of the Naga kingdom came into view below them. The Moonbird and the turtle both spread their wings and glided over the city. Madai was awed by the gleaming spires and domes that crowned the massive towers. They hovered over a vast courtyard of intricately arranged pearls.

"*Beh!*" cried Madai with surprise when he glimpsed his first Nagas marching across the courtyard, with the hoods and fangs of cobras, the faces, arms, and torsos of humans, and the immense serpentine bodies of dragons. The Nagas carried drums and flutes in a massive and sonorous funeral procession.

They landed at the edge of the courtyard, which was ringed with pagodas and pyramids of delicately carved black coral, inlaid with mother-of-pearl friezes of ancient Naga myths. The buildings seemed as tall as mountains to Madai, who had never seen any larger than a thatched village temple. Their golden rooftiles glimmered in the rippling light that had no apparent source. The limpid atmosphere had qualities of both air and water—Madai could float, and also breathe—or not, as he wished.

The Naga procession filled the courtyard with cacophonous music, to send the soul of Basudara, the dead King, on its journey to the mountain in the center of the universe. A gnarled old Naga, wearing the knotted cord of a Brahman priest, sat on an elegant ebony platform surrounded by palm-leaf banners, reciting the archaic Sanskrit funeral incantations. Incense smoke rose from filigreed braziers. The Naga priest rang his bell, and tossed holy water and fragrant yellow tampaka blossoms at the procession. Four younger Naga priests read the history of the Naga kings from palm-leaf texts.

Now a great ship with elaborate patterns of crimson and gold sailed into the plaza, carrying ornate baskets of offerings, and the immediate family of the deceased Naga King. Lesser relatives followed the vessel, chanting prayers so the dead soul would glide on peaceful waters to the far shore, then rise like a butterfly to the central mountain, where ancestral spirits dwell.

Madai noticed a lovely Naga female at the prow of the boat, her head wreathed in a flaring cobra hood adorned with pearls, cradling a young Naga in her arms. The Naga woman glanced in their direction with luminous, slitted eyes, but her child didn't follow his mother's gaze—because he was blind. He had no eyes at all.

"That is Mahanagini, the Naga Queen," explained the Moonbird.

"Her son is heir to Basudara's throne, but when he was very small he mischievously crushed the head of a sea snail, whose father was a powerful Raksa demon that cursed the prince with blindness. The lad has never grown or regained his sight since then—many lifetimes ago, according to your reckoning."

Madai thought guiltily of all the sea snails he'd idly crushed.

"All the relatives of the dead King are quarreling over who will inherit the throne," added Bedawang. "I fear that certain factions will try to harm the blind prince and his mother."

Now the cremation tower entered the courtyard, carried by a retinue of hundreds of chanting Nagas with peaked headdresses and ornate kris daggers with sharp, wavy blades. The tower was a rattan platform supported by long, thin bamboo poles, covered with tier upon tier of colorful brocade umbrellas, topped with a gilt spire. On the platform stood a huge wooden water buffalo, which contained the corpse of the Naga King. The bull was black, with long golden horns twined with flowers, and detailed golden designs adorning its body. Its eyes were great red orbs, and there was a bundle of straw in its mouth. The platform was placed in the center of the courtyard.

A line of cobra-hooded female Nagas with gilt and flowered headdresses slithered across the plaza carrying lavish offerings of succulent seafoods in wicker baskets, which they heaped beneath the water buffalo effigy. The Naga musicians played their drums and flutes with stately rhythms, and the spear holders began a sinuous dance, raising and lowering their glittering krises with graceful gestures.

A Naga priest entered with a flaming torch that somehow burned in this aquatic realm. The music pounded, and the sword dancers swayed and whirled. The priest ignited the straw in the water buffalo's mouth with the torch, and the cremation fire sprang up, emitting thick black smoke. A flow of red and black engulfed the water buffalo, which became a glowing framework containing the huge smoking coffin. The sword dancers poked at the fire so it would burn more fiercely. The ceremonial umbrellas ignited, a sheet of flame rose up, and the legs of the water buffalo began to collapse. Yet Madai felt no heat, because they were under the sea.

Suddenly a band of spear holders bellowed, and broke away from the formation at the flaming tower. They rushed to the ritual boat and slithered aboard, their long dragon tails twitching furiously. They surrounded the terrified Naga Queen and her little blind son, shoving aside relatives and servants who tried to aid them. Moving as fast as vipers, they dragged the struggling Queen and her child from the ceremonial ship, and tossed them onto the flaming mass of the funeral pyre. The Queen flared her cobra hood and uttered one long wail.

The loyal kris dancers struggled to reach them, but the rebel faction ringed the pyre and held them back. There was silence in the courtyard, except for the clash of weapons, the grunts of battling Nagas, and the crackle of flames.

Then two winged figures rose up from the courtyard and dipped into the inferno. The Queen slithered onto the Moonbird's back, while Bedawang gently lifted the blind Naga prince with his parrot-like beak. The two flying creatures rose above the crumbling pyre and circled over the plaza.

The rebels shouted and hurled their gilded krises at the gliding figures. Then they were engulfed by a wave of loyalist Naga soldiers, and the elaborate patterns of the courtyard grew slippery with dark Naga blood.

"Don't forget me!" shouted Madai, terrified of being abandoned in this eerie place.

The Moonbird dipped again, and Madai clambered onto its back, behind the Naga Queen. The enraged rebels roared at the Garuda, but the Moonbird soared above the golden pagodas.

Mahanagini, the Naga Queen, sat sideways, like a European horsewoman. Her graceful arms clasped the Moonbird's neck, and her sinewy, iridescent dragon tail coiled beneath them.

They followed the winged turtle up . . . up . . . until the Naga kingdom could no longer be seen and there was only the silent dark. Madai held tightly on to the cool, scaly shoulders of the Queen to keep his balance. He was frightened of plunging into the void.

They deposited the Queen and her son in an isolated undersea grotto, where they could wait until Bedawang summoned her soldiers to fetch them. With a grateful smile, she plucked a large, glowing pearl from her headdress and gave it to Madai, who accepted it with a bow.

"How long have we been gone; is it late in the day?" he asked the Moonbird when they were finally alone in the comforting familiarity of the coral reef.

"A day of Brama is a *kalpa* of 4,320 million earthly years," explained the Moonbird. "Within each kalpa are cycles of 306,720,000 years. Each cycle contains seventy-one eons divided into four ages.

Your island is currently in the age of Kali, so it isn't very late in the Brama day."

"You mean ages and eons have passed!" cried Madai.

"No time has passed on your island. The Naga kingdom intersects the earthly timeline, and however long we lingered in the gilded city, your sun remained fixed in your sky. Don't fret, it's still early in your morning. There's still plenty of daylight for fishing."

6

"That's wonderful, Madai," beamed his mother when she saw the basket of fresh seafood. "Look Bapak, our boy has become a diver!"

"Hey, boy," laughed his father, slapping him on the back. "You look tired from diving all day. Have a beer. I thought you'd run to the mission to become a priest when you didn't go out in the boat. Let's fry the catch in coco-oil. Madai's a real man now—we'll have a feast!"

His younger brother, Ketut, eyed the shellfish greedily.

His petite older sister, Dawan, came into the house carrying a bundle of clean laundry on her head. She had cared for Madai during his sickly childhood, fondly carrying him around the village on her hip, so they were very close.

"You've been down at the pond, bathing and doing laundry with Lasmi and the other girls?" Madai asked.

"Yes," Dawan smiled. "Why? Are you keeping an eye on Lasmi? You always walk and laugh with her—you hardly ever tell me things anymore. I see you've finally become a fisherman. Preparing to start a family for yourself?"

Madai's tired face flushed and his relatives laughed.

They busied themselves around the cooking fire, frying the fish and stirring the curried rice. As she cooked, his mother chattered about events and gossip in the tight-knit desa community.

There was still some daylight before supper, so Madai decided to take a basket of lobsters to Lasmi and her widowed mother, who lived in a small wicker cottage on the village outskirts. Not too many lobsters—he didn't want it misinterpreted as a courting gift. He wasn't ready for that yet.

At sixteen he was old enough. Nearly half the boys in his age group were already married—and the other half were looking. But Madai had his own ideas about that, just like everything else. He would wait. It wasn't time for him to start a family yet.

He couldn't be like a mission priest and remain alone all his life, and when the time came it would be with Lasmi. They had playfully kissed and fondled under a grove of mangosteen trees during the last full-moon festival, and he loved her—but he wasn't ready to marry yet.

He'd asked the Moonbird, and the shimmering Garuda sternly replied, "If you become too mature and burdened with responsibilities, you'll grow too heavy for me to carry."

That cooled his ardor. He didn't want to lose the Moonbird, yet he didn't want to lose Lasmi either. If he waited too long, someone who was older and stronger, more rich and powerful would certainly take her. The men already watched her admiringly when she walked through the village in a bright batik sarong, tall and high-breasted, with thick black hair. Just recently the wealthy widower Ram had sent her a gift of rice.

It wasn't just her beauty that drew Madai. He loved to talk to her. She was his second cousin and had always been his best friend. He couldn't tell anyone about the Moonbird, but she enjoyed the books at the mission school. He could share the enthusiasm and wonder of his discoveries with her. She was excited by men walking on the moon, pills that cure sickness, and machines that do the work of people.

They pored over mildewed old issues of the *National Geographic* together, exclaiming with surprise at what they saw. Sometimes they talked about going to the swarming capital on Java together, to study at the big university.

Yet they both knew this was a hopeless fantasy. They came from poor desa families that planted, fished, and gathered, and sold their wood carvings and handicrafts to the big hotels on Bali. They could barely afford kerosene for their lamps, or petrol for the outboard motors of their dugouts. They could never afford the university on the main island. That was for the rich.

Lasmi knew it was an idle dream, so she saw no reason to wait. Sometimes she teased Madai, caressing him and taunting him about becoming a lonely old priest.

She couldn't hear the words of the Moonbird echoing in his mind, *"If you become too mature and burdened with responsibilities, you'll grow too heavy for me to carry."*

Lasmi couldn't understand why Madai wanted to wait. They loved each other and were old enough to marry. She enjoyed sharing his science books and *National Geographics*, and talking about exciting modern lands. But she knew they'd never really have the money to go anywhere.

She also knew that Madai was a strange and moody loner. He often drove her away when he took his solitary sojourns into the forest—where the villagers sometimes came upon him sitting and dreaming, nodding and mumbling.

She complained about these things in her outspoken way, and he knew they made her unhappy. He knew that if he waited too long he'd lose her to another, simpler—or richer—man. Yet he must wait —if he wanted to keep the Moonbird.

Lasmi's father had drowned at sea one night long ago, when the cruel and mysterious lantern ship lured him beyond the protective coral reef. She lived with her mother and younger sister in a worn wicker compound at the seaward edge of the desa—a neighborhood frequented by pigs and leyak spirits. Madai wandered along the muddy pathway to their house.

Lasmi's mother was also a tall woman, with one lame leg, and a face that was worn but still handsome. She sat with her daughters outside their shabby house preparing a skimpy evening meal.

"Madai son," she smiled warmly when she saw him, revealing few remaining teeth. "Have you come to marry my daughter?"

Lasmi flushed and her little sister giggled.

"No, Ibu, but I brought you some lobsters." He grinned.

The older woman's eyes gleamed as she accepted the basket. "So you've become a diver! Perhaps my eldest daughter isn't so foolish, refusing a rich widower to wait for you."

While her mother cleaned the shellfish, Lasmi and Madai wandered hand in hand to a secluded grove of banana trees behind the house. Lasmi hugged and embraced him—but he pulled away.

"What's wrong, Madai?" she demanded. "I'm almost fifteen and I can't wait too long for you. My mother says I'm at the peak of my beauty now. Wealthy widower Ram wants me to live at his house. I don't love him but he's not so bad; he can buy me bangles and shoes, and food for my family. I love you, Madai, but I can't wait forever. I don't care if you're not rich, we can live on your damn lobsters. I want to be your wife—why don't you want me?"

"Let's wait, Lasmi. I love you, but if we marry, then we must always stay here in the desa. There'll be no hope for anything more. We'll never go to the university or see modern cities. We'll spend the rest of our lives on the island, breeding like chickens."

Lasmi grew angry. "You fool, we'll spend the rest of our lives here anyway, whether we breed like chickens or not! How will we ever get away to exciting places—by selling carvings to tourists? I'm going to marry nice old widower Ram."

Lasmi kicked and slapped at him with frustration, and they fought and struggled. Then they felt sorry and kissed longingly.

Madai knew he wasn't being fair with Lasmi, wasn't telling her what was really on his mind. Lately he'd wondered if the Moonbird could carry him to Bali. Maybe the eagle god could even fly as far as Djakarta—or Australia.

But if he left the island, he'd leave Lasmi behind—and if he remained here caressing her, he'd succumb eventually and never go anywhere. It was confusing.

One thing might please her—the Naga Queen's pearl. But when Madai proudly fished it from his carrying pouch, he found only a small brown pebble. He stared at it in his hand.

Lasmi's mother hobbled into the banana grove to fetch them. "Come stir the curry so it doesn't burn, Lasmi, and slice up the fish. Supper is almost ready. What's the matter, Madai, you look so pale. You mustn't tire yourself out diving for too many lobsters."

In the depths of the banana grove, the big white ape with the oddly clipped tail crouched, peeling fruit and watching Madai with wise, probing eyes.

One night the Moonbird unexpectedly whispered into his mind, "The lantern ship is here, do you want to see it?"

Madai felt a ripple of fear. The lantern ship came at rare intervals, but always during a new moon. It sailed far out along the horizon at night, with its flashing blue lanterns beckoning hypnotically.

Fishermen who saw the lantern ship from the shore yearned to sail out to greet it. The lantern ship lured them farther and farther out to sea—until the boatmen were lost beyond the barrier reef and never returned.

That was how Lasmi's father had drowned.

The lantern ship would be sailing tonight, and Madai could ride the Moonbird to see it, without any danger of being trapped by the riptides beyond the protective coral reef.

They flew to the shore and landed on a large outcropping of sandstone, where the muddy green river enters the sea. It was a black night. The river was a dark flow, while the sea shone opaline purple under the stars, with a sparkling of phosphorescent algae beneath the surface.

A pretty sight, but the women who stood on the flimsy wooden docks at the edge of the windy, rocky promontory weren't enjoying the view. They were weeping and clutching with tense white knuckles at the men who stood beside them.

"Don't sail out to the lantern ship," they implored the fishermen. "Or you'll never come back to the land."

The eyes of the men strained eagerly to the horizon, where the distant chain of pale blue lights bobbed cheerily up and down. Madai felt the compulsion himself—suddenly he longed to race out and see what rode on that ship.

"Don't worry," the fishermen impatiently soothed their women. "We won't go out too far—just a little ways. We'll stay inside the reef, promise, and come back to pester you soon. The lantern ship doesn't look so far out tonight. Heard there's treasure on board. Just like to see for ourselves."

Madai watched from the rocks. He knew that when he was perched on the Moonbird nobody could see them. The men launched their triangular-sailed outriggers, whose colorful fish-faced prows had brightly painted, staring eyes to frighten leyaks.

"Hurry!" said Madai. "Let's fly out there."

They glided across the water to the inviting string of gaily bobbing blue lights. Madai felt the same irresistible curiosity as all the men on the island. He *had* to see what it was! Treasure, maybe. Leyak-spirits, maybe. Lost sailors, maybe. He didn't care, he had to know what rode the lantern ship.

The night was still and warm, and the glowing Garuda soared on the air currents. The purple sea glistened beneath them and the blue lights of the lantern ship beckoned and called just up ahead . . . Just a little farther out . . .

There it was! Madai peered down over the luminous wings of the Moonbird. He saw a broad, dark raft strung with festive blue lanterns. But the raft seemed empty. There were no treasure chests, no spirits or sailors. Nothing.

There was a sudden movement near the center of the raft. A form was stirring, and in the blue lamplight Madai could see a face staring up at them—framed in a tangle of long, copper hair. The face was white and tusked, with huge, cold eyes. A trembling hand with long nails lifted and gestured to them.

"Rangda!" cried Madai in surprise.

The eyes flickered and the mouth smiled slightly. Then the face lowered into tangled hair, and disappeared into the dark mass of the gaily lit raft.

"It's Rangda the Sorceress! We must warn the fishermen or she'll drown them all—fly back to shore," he urged Moonbird.

But the bright little dugouts were already sailing out to the hypnotic blue lights on the horizon.

The shadowy flicker reappeared. The white tusked face looked up at him amidst coppery hair . . . The sneering eyes . . . The faint smile . . . The trembling claws beckoned.

"What do you want?" cried Madai.

A voice hissed in the deepest part of his mind. "Rangda can show you . . ."

"What do you mean? Go away!"

"Rangda can show you what you must see."

"I don't want to see anything."

"Sail with Rangda tonight . . . She'll show you so many things."

"No!"

"See," hissed Rangda.

The raft dissolved before Madai's eyes, and he saw a plump village mama just waking up to light the fire for morning rice gruel.

"*See,*" hissed Rangda.

As Madai watched, horrified, the stout body of the woman began to age and fester. She seemed unaware of what was happening to her as she scratched her head and yawned, wrapped a faded old cotton sarong around her waist, and shooed the chickens from a rack of drying lychee fruit. Then she began to collect small sticks of firewood and coco-husks.

All the while her body was dissolving. Great runny wounds cracked open on her face and body. The flesh of her legs rotted as she walked, into a red mass of protruding bones.

"Stop it!" cried Madai.

"*See,*" hissed the voice in his mind. "She'll be dead before the moon is gone. There is no way to stop it."

"Stop it!" screamed Madai. "Help me, Moonbird!"

"See," hissed the flickering white tusked face amidst the long tangle of hair. "It goes on and on and never stops. I do not cause it, nothing *causes* it. It goes on and on . . . See."

In a delirious semidream, Madai watched the hideous procession of Rangda's cursed victims that appeared before him. Dead bodies, half decayed. Drowned bodies, bloated and white. Sick bodies, shaking with fever. Weak and aged bodies, withered and misshapen.

Was it really Rangda that caused these things, Madai wondered, or the missionaries' devil? Maybe it was karmic vengeance or merely random chance. Madai couldn't know.

But now it was Rangda who entranced his mind and trapped it in a horrible embrace, so that Madai couldn't avoid the endless march of misery and decay. He twisted and writhed, trying to wrench away from Rangda's grasp.

"*See,*" hissed the witch, fondling the pale corpse of a stillborn infant in her clawed hands.

Madai saw people with wounds and burns . . . People with blood and scars. "Moonbird!" he cried. "Help me, Moonbird."

Suddenly everything changed. The breeze blew warm and silky, and the sweet scent of frangipani flowers filled the air. In Madai's delirium, he saw the peaceful desa community in the morning.

Villagers laughed and gossiped as they ate their rice gruel. The temple dancers moved with lithe grace, rehearsing for the next festival. Gecko lizards chirped and scuttled on the mossy sandstone icons. Big red papayas grew ripe on the trees, and the mangoes were heavy and sweet. The fishermen joked as they strolled to their dugouts, the women talked as they tended their fertile rice paddies, and children scampered to the mission school. Lasmi, Dawan, and the young village women giggled and chattered as they bathed and did laundry in the pond. A kitten chased bits of fluff.

"This also goes on and on," whispered the Moonbird soothingly. "Don't be afraid."

The air grew foggy and cold, and there was a rumble of thunder in the overcast sky. The fish-headed sailboats capsized in the high surf beyond the reef as they tried to reach the lantern ship.

"This also goes on and on," sneered Rangda, holding the dead baby against her withered breast.

The white-robed temple priests led a noisy funeral procession to the cremation grounds. The widow and orphans sobbed while greedy relatives haggled over their inheritance, and musicians played a funeral dirge on their reed flutes. Beetles attacked a grove of lychee trees as foul, greasy smoke filled the air.

"It never stops," hissed Rangda, tossing the corpse of the stillborn infant onto the raft, and shaking her long, copper hair.

Warm sunshine glistened on clear water, and a silvery school of flying fish arced through the air. The children whispered and giggled in the mission school, and the young women at the pond gracefully scrubbed each other's backs. Madai's mother and younger brother, Ketut, laughed at the antics of the kitten. The women tending the paddies said the rice crop would be abundant this year. The sinuous festival dancers rehearsed to melodious music and the geckos chirped softly in the sunshine. Two lovers caressed.

"It goes on so peacefully," whispered Moonbird.

Lightning flashed through the cold air. A high wave struck the fishing boat of three young brothers beyond the reef, and their outrigger was swamped and overturned. A rattan cookhouse caught fire when a toddler knocked over a pot of smoldering coals. A viper bit a little girl who was picking passion fruit in the forest, and beetles wiped out the entire lychee crop. Madai's old aunt Mai had stomach pains.

"*See,*" hissed Rangda, kicking the corpse of the infant into the sea and smiling slightly. "The misery never stops."

The gentle winds blew through the orchid-twined mango trees, and the fruit grew fat and sweet. Handsome white egrets fished along the river and ardent frogs clamored. The young women at the pond sang wistful love songs as they scrubbed the clothes on the rocks. Madai's mother smiled as she pounded rice and curry spices for their supper.

"The people are happy," whispered Moonbird.

Madai was unable to wrench his mind from the terrible battle between Moonbird the Protector, servant of Visnu the Preserver; and Rangda the Sorceress, servant of Siva the Destroyer. The visions in his mind shifted back and forth from misery and despair to pleasure and happiness.

"*Stop* it," he cried. "I don't want to see *any* of this. I just want to go reef fishing!"

"*See,*" hissed Rangda. And the island grew cold and ugly, filled with hate and pain, death and decay.

"Don't be frightened," whispered the Moonbird. And the island grew warm and joyous, full of love and play.

The two beings fought for Madai's mind until he could no longer stand it—and still they battled on.

"Why do you hate the people?" Madai cried to Rangda. "Why do you torment them?"

"I don't hate these people—they harass me," hissed Rangda, her mouth twisted with anger. "I wasn't always such a hag, once I was young and pleasing to see. I was espoused to the sovereign of Bali, and bore a son and a beauteous daughter. My son was destined to be Raja. The girl and I studied talismans and medicinal herbs. When my husband perished, I was supposed to incinerate myself on his cremation pyre. Widows were accursed in those days. My sweet daughter persuaded me to resist, so I swallowed herbs of invisibility to escape the fires. The priests said I was a sorceress, so I was banished to the forests, where vicious tigers skulk. My steadfast daughter came with me—we survived exile through our sorcery. Soon all misfortunes in that place were ascribed to me. Years passed and the rebellious Brahmans were banished from Bali, so we sailed in their vessels to this isolated isle—seeking refuge. The Raja of these simple folks accepted us and asked to wed my graceful princess—until the detestable priests and this verminous fowl whispered that we practiced sorcery, so we were banished to the forests once again. We must sleep amidst nests of scorpions and vipers, and listen to vicious songs which say that all misery and disease are caused by me. *I do not cause, I only see!* Soar away now, but you have seen—sorrow goes on endlessly. Soon you'll understand what you shall see. Rangda waits to show you . . . see."

The witch's grisly face sank down on the dark raft, and Madai's mind was freed. The lustrous wings of the Moonbird spread wide to catch the air currents, and they glided away from the bobbing blue lights of the lantern ship.

"What happened?" Madai groaned.

"Rangda is jealous. She wants you for herself," said Moonbird.

"Keep her away from me. I hate her—she causes nothing but trouble."

"She says she *causes* nothing, that she only reveals what will inevitably happen."

"Wherever Rangda looks, something terrible occurs. Keep her away."

"I have known her for a long time and she is very powerful," whispered the Garuda.

"What about the fishermen who sailed out to the lantern ship?" asked Madai. "Let's fly out and see what happened to them."

They flew low over the water, looking for bright-eyed fishing boats still afloat in the wild surf beyond the protective coral reef. There was no sign of any survivors in the black sea.

Madai scanned the water with his flashlight. "Look!" he shouted.

Below them was a capsized dugout bucking in the rough waves while three young brothers clutched at its slippery sides.

"Turn the boat upright with your beak!" said Madai to the Moonbird.

The Garuda glanced at him with surprised iridescent eyes. "We cannot change the course of the future," it whispered.

"Yes we can," insisted Madai. "Turn the boat over, they can't hold on much longer."

"So be it," said the Moonbird, dipping down abruptly.

"*Beh!*" cried the brothers as the boat magically flipped upright. They clambered back into their dugout.

Madai chuckled softly. He was invisible when he rode the Moonbird—this could be fun.

The little boat was still in the dangerous rough waters beyond the reef.

"Let's nudge it back to safety," said Madai.

The Moonbird used its curved beak to push the colorful boat back into the calm waters of the cove. The three astonished brothers chanted to the gods as the unseen force propelled them toward the shore.

Madai bounced with excitement on the Moonbird's back. "Let's find the others!"

They searched the churning surf most of that night, but the other fishermen could not be found. They had flown like butterflies to the far shore. To the mountain in the center of the universe where the spirits of ancestors dwell.

II

Madai learned to use his powers . . .

8

One night, shortly before his eighteenth birthday, Madai had a frightening dream. He saw his younger brother, Ketut, walking in the forest, wearing a short sarong and humming to himself. His thin, tawny arms carried a wicker basket for picking wild mushrooms.

At Ketut's feet something stirred in the tall grass. There was a hiss and a flicker, and Madai saw a white tusked face, a tangle of coppery hair glinting in the sunlight, and a trembling, clawed hand.

"*See,*" said a hoarse voice.

Then Ketut's body burst into smoky flames, and quickly burned to a pile of charred rubble—just like a cremation tower. Madai woke from the dream with a muffled cry, and found his own body bathed with sweat.

Yet Ketut seemed lively and cheerful as usual over the morning rice gruel, and Madai gradually forgot the dream. Until several days later, when he and the Moonbird were plucking shellfish from the peaceful depths of the sea.

The Moonbird paused and listened intently.

"What's wrong?" asked Madai.

"We must fly quickly," said the Garuda.

They sailed into the air, leaving a nearly full basket of surprised lobsters behind, and flew over the forest. There was Ketut in his short, flowered sarong, carrying his basket and humming—as a small green viper darted from the tall grass with a flicker and a hiss, and sank its fangs in the flesh just above Ketut's ankle.

"*Beh!*" cried Ketut.

"Why do you tread upon the viperfolk, man-child?" spat the viper. "I have bruised your heel, but did you not almost crush my head as you walked heedlessly through the grasses? Certainly it is so . . ." Then the green viper slithered away.

The birds rose up from the bamboo grove and shrieked to one another that a human child had been waylaid by one of the viperfolk. The frogs basking in a nearby pond added their voices to the confusion, and even the banyan tree sighed.

Ketut stood silently in the pathway, staring at his injured leg. Then he sank dizzily to his knees, dropping his basket of mushrooms, which scattered in every direction. He examined his ankle, which was already puffing up with a throbbing, purplish swelling around the wound. The viper had injected its venom into two deep punctures in his skin.

He knew what to do, for every child raised on the island is trained in such matters. He took a small, sharp knife from a pouch at his slight waist, and with trembling hands sliced deeply into his own flesh, directly through the bite marks.

Blood mixed with milky venom oozed from the cut. Now he should walk slowly to the village, stopping only to rest and cut into the wound again, to express more of the venom. But Ketut seemed dazed. Instead of rising to his feet and walking, he remained crouched down, staring in shock at his swollen, bleeding ankle.

"The venom is spreading into his system," said Madai. "We must do something or he'll die!"

"The leaf drops in its own time," said the Moonbird.

"No!" insisted Madai. "We *must* help him. You carry Ketut back to the village and I'll follow on foot."

"He cannot see me—there is no way I can carry him."

Madai pondered for a moment. "You can carry me under the sea without breath—can you take me into the wound to clean up the venom?"

"It isn't as simple as catching shellfish," whispered the Moonbird.

"I don't care if it's simple—is it possible?"

"Most things are possible, but it's very dangerous."

"I don't care if it's dangerous," said Madai. "Let's try."

The Moonbird spread its wings and swooped toward the ground. Then suddenly—Madai was never quite sure how it happened—they were inside the jagged tunnel of the fang bite—and inside Ketut's flesh.

It was still and peaceful, like underwater, and it resembled a picture in a science book. Bunches of long red muscle fibers pulsed all around them, twined with tubules carrying blood, and flashing strands of nerves. Madai looked around in wonder, but there was no time to admire the view. The milky mucus of the viper's venom, heavily tinged with blood, flowed through the landscape like the fiery lava of a volcano—destroying everything in its pathway.

Where the venom touched live muscle and nerve fibers, they shriveled and curled into brittle, ashy gray. The venom ate its way like acid into the blood vessels, and burst the blood cells like bubbles. Then it traveled up the vessels toward other parts of Ketut's body, burning and bursting wherever it touched.

"What can we do?" frowned Madai.

"What does your mother do when coco-milk is spilled on the straw sleeping mats?" asked the Moonbird.

"She wipes it up with some old rag—do you think I can mop up the venom with my sarong?"

"You can try."

Madai leaped off the back of the Moonbird, tore strips of cloth from the edge of his sarong, and sponged up the puddles of reddened, milky venom from inside his brother's wound. He tried not to get it on his feet and hands, stepping carefully around the puddles and mopping gingerly, but it was impossible to prevent the viper's poisons from touching his own skin—and wherever it touched, painful red welts appeared.

Yet Madai hardly noticed, he was so intent on his work. He tore the strips of cloth from his sarong one by one, and slowly, painstakingly used them to absorb the toxins from Ketut's flesh before they spread. As he busily tore and mopped, the Moonbird stood silently nearby on a mound of ligament.

Gradually . . . Very gradually the puddles of bloody venom began to diminish, dissolving the strips of cloth into shreds of fiber—instead of dissolving Ketut's tissues. Madai tore and sponged, unaware of anything else until he suddenly slipped in a mushy pool of blood, venom, and cellular debris, and fell against a sheath of damaged muscle fibers that tore abruptly, and sent him thrashing and reeling backward with a yelp.

With effortless calm, the Moonbird stretched its long neck and pinned Madai with its beak, setting him upright. Where his back had grazed against the venom-slicked muscle, there arose a long, painful welt.

"You're beginning to tire," observed the Moonbird. "But look around. The big puddles of venom are gone. There are just a few cavities where the muck has collected. Clean them up quickly so we can leave this painful, dank place. Your brother's ankle has been badly damaged and will take a while to mend, but there's no longer enough poison to threaten his life."

Madai shook with weariness and the pain of the welts, yet he worked stubbornly until the last of the slushy venom was wiped away, leaving a nasty, jagged wound in his brother's ankle.

Madai clambered onto the Moonbird, and rested his whirling head against the cool moonstone feathers. The Moonbird rose up, out of Ketut's body, into the diffuse sunlight of the forest.

They watched with relief as Ketut gradually recovered from the effects of the toxin, regained his senses, and slowly hobbled down the grassy pathway toward the desa.

"How can it be that the viper's sting did not destroy the manchild?" shrieked a flock of blue parakeets in a big old mango tree.

The mosquitoes swarmed around Ketut's leg, drawn by the scent of his blood, and buzzed with wordless bewilderment.

They followed Ketut until he was safely home, but Madai couldn't rest yet. He felt a great wave of excitement and whooped with elation as they soared above the forest. "You can take me anywhere," he shouted to the Moonbird. "I'll bet you can even fly to the moon!"

"The moon is a harsh and inhospitable place," said the Garuda. "Are you ready for such a difficult journey?"

"You mean you really *can* fly to the moon?" asked Madai, surprised anew by such magic—he'd merely been teasing.

"I can fly anyplace that you can envision."

"Then take me to the moon—I want to walk like a spaceman on the moon!"

"You won't find any lobsters there," observed the Moonbird, reminding Madai of his father. "But if we are lucky, we can obtain some moon-milk to heal the welts on your skin."

The Moonbird began to ascend almost vertically. The steamy forest dwindled to a green blur far below them. They broke through a bank of feathery clouds and the ground below could no longer be seen. They continued to move upward, a shimmering dot in the deep sapphire sky, crowned by the blazing sun. As they ascended, the blue of the sky darkened into blackness, and the curve of the earth appeared below them.

It looked like pictures Madai had seen in the *National Geographic*, with swirling masses of clouds forming patterns that veiled the lapis blue seas and the jade archipelago of little islands. Other areas stood out in bold, cloudless contrast. Madai thought he could see the coast of Australia, a reddish land mass far to the south.

They rose upward in the deeply cold, airless night, and the flashing patterns of the stars inflamed Madai's excitement. Now the moon itself loomed large in the foreground while the earth hovered distantly below, half its face shining in sunlight while the other half was shrouded by night.

They floated above the luminous gray surface of the moon, pockmarked with craters of every size. They drifted down to a plain that was strewn with boulders and a dense layer of rock fragments. The profoundly frigid, lifeless dark frightened Madai, and he knew that if he were separated from the Moonbird for even a moment he couldn't survive. Island boys cannot walk barefoot on the moon.

"Nearby is the lake of moon-milk," said the Garuda. "Cool moon-milk streams through the night, and refreshes all the plants and animals of earth after they have been scorched and dried by the heat of the sun. The gods and demons sip from the lake to gain immortality. It's too powerful a drink for you, but I can spread some on your skin to soothe your wounds—if we can reach the lake."

"Is it hidden?" asked Madai.

"No, it's easy to find, but the demons who visit that spot are very fierce—and you are very frail. If you slip off my back you will die in an instant."

Madai shivered. He didn't want to die in an instant in this bleak place. Let the bold Americans walk on the moon.

The Garuda lifted its wings and skimmed along the rough, glowing lunar surface, over strange, twisted rock formations, circular craters and oddly shaped gorges, dead seas and tortuous ranges of hills. Finally Madai spotted the glimmering lake of translucent moon-milk.

There was little chance to enjoy its beauty, for on the horizon there appeared an immense, disembodied head, with sunken, emaciated cheeks and an enormous, slavering mouth. The head was entirely bald, its eyes burned like charcoals, and the hollow planes of the face gleamed like moonlight. It was the mouth that made the face so monstrous, with wet, swollen lips, jagged yellow teeth, and a long, dripping red tongue that wagged to and fro with restless hunger.

"That is the Titan, Rahu," said the Moonbird. "In the earliest moments of your world he stole the first sip of moon-milk to gain immortality. The god Visnu was furious that a mere Titan had pushed ahead of the gods to drink the elixir, so he beheaded Rahu with one stroke of his jeweled kris dagger. Because the drink had passed through the Titan's mouth and throat, the head became immortal, while the severed body quickly decayed. Rahu's head will live forever, craving only one thing—another sip of moon-milk."

"What prevents him from drinking from the lake?" asked Madai.

"Nothing prevents him," said the Moonbird. "But he has no stomach to hold it. He drinks and drinks, but it passes right through his throat, and he feels more and more feverish with thirst. At times he becomes so frustrated that he swallows up the entire moon with his gaping mouth, but it just slips out again through his gullet. When Rahu swallows the moon, the earthfolk see a lunar eclipse. Rahu is a sad creature. He cannot die, but he can never attain peace. His long tongue laps ceaselessly at the lake of moon-milk, but he has no body to retain the elixir, so he never feels refreshed."

"What a miserable being," said Madai.

"Miserable and dangerous too," said the Moonbird. "For he guards the lake jealously, and challenges any god, demon or Titan who tries to enjoy it."

"Maybe I don't need moon-milk to heal my welts," said Madai nervously. "Maybe we should go back to the desa and ask a wandering herb-woman for a poultice."

"Those welts weren't caused by natural means, and no natural remedy will heal them."

At that moment the head spotted them, and rolled swiftly across the rubbled surface of the moon like a giant ball, until it came to rest just beneath them.

"What do you and your scrawny companion want, Sparrow-God?" wheezed the disembodied Titan.

"We want only a small portion of moon-milk to heal this earthchild's wounds."

"I guard the lake and you may not touch it."

"My master Visnu taught you the peril of insatiable greed—must I teach you the lesson again?" asked the Moonbird.

"You, Chicken-God?" Rahu's wheezing voice aped a grotesque laugh. "I'll teach you not to trespass where you're not welcome."

The two spirits traded insults and seemed to be gearing up for battle—Madai wanted to go home.

Rahu struck first, darting his long tongue upward and wrapping it around the Moonbird's leg like a noose, pulling the Garuda to the rough lunar surface—then gobbling at the Moonbird's legs with slimy, jagged teeth.

The Moonbird lunged at Rahu's eye with its beak, and popped it like a berry. The Titan bawled with pain—but the eye re-formed immediately because it was immortal.

Rahu had devoured the Moonbird's legs and was gobbling his way up the Garuda's body. Madai felt genuinely terrified. Even if the monster couldn't digest them, he could certainly crush them with those hideously powerful teeth. He curled up into a trembling little ball on the Moonbird's back.

Then the Garuda did a surprising thing. Instead of battling the Titan—he slipped past the gnashing teeth and down Rahu's throat—which was thickly coated with moon-milk. The Moonbird twisted and turned lithely inside Rahu's gullet, so that droplets of moon-milk formed a glowing nimbus around Madai.

Rahu tried to cough them back up—to reach them with his pulverizing jaws, but the Moonbird slid gracefully down from the Titan's throat and soared up into the black lunar sky, dominated by a lustrous earth-arc.

Rahu squalled with rage, for he knew he'd been tricked. Madai uncurled and sat proudly upright on the Moonbird, surrounded by a luminous halo of moon-milk, which soothed and healed the welts caused by the viper's venom.

Then Madai and the Moonbird sailed across the resplendent sky, a tiny speck of radiance moving like a shooting star, down into the humid mists and forests of earth.

9

When Madai wearily returned home, he found Ketut weeping and complaining about pain in his ankle, which was swollen and angry red.

Their mother fussed over him, spooning coco-milk into his mouth. "Where have you been all day?" she cried when she saw Madai. "Your brother was bit by a viper! It's a wonder he didn't die. And look at you—your sarong is all torn and there are little scratches on your skin."

"I slipped and fell in the coral, Ibu, I lost my basket of lobsters."

"No matter, so long as you aren't hurt. Who can think about supper when your brother is so sick?"

The next morning Ketut was feverish and his ankle was hugely swollen. By the afternoon he was delirious and his skin burned to the touch.

"The wound is festering," said their father. "We'll call in an herb doctor, and take him to the temple for healing prayers."

But Madai knew that the wound was infected, and Ketut was too sick for any herbs or prayers. He grew sicker by the hour, and lay on his mat blazing with fever, and dehydrated because he could hold no cooling fluids.

Madai lay awake on his sleeping mat that night, listening to his brother moaning and tossing with pain. There was no denying what he must do.

He rose up before dawn and went to the marshy clearing amidst the banyans and bamboos, and summoned the Moonbird with the beam of his flashlight. When the iridescent Garuda appeared he said simply, "You must show me how to heal sickness."

"It's risky," whispered the Moonbird.

"I'm not afraid of the risks. Show me how."

"Climb on my back."

Madai climbed onto the shimmering Moonbird. There was the familiar tensing of large muscles and the rustling of wings. They flew low over the forest, to the desa and Madai's family compound.

Then somehow they dipped inside the sleeping house and hovered over the body of Ketut, who writhed with fever on his mat.

Then they reentered Ketut's flesh.

Madai flicked on his flashlight, and again he saw the eerie internal landscape of bundled muscle fibers, laced with flashing strands of nerves and tubular blood vessels. There were no more puddles of venom. Instead countless minute globular creatures formed grapelike clusters that clung to every surface and multiplied with wild abandon.

Wherever the loathsome clusters hung, they had poisoned the tissues inside Ketut's ankle, which had the look—and stench—of rotten meat. The miniscule creatures fed off the decaying flesh while endlessly dividing and doubling their numbers.

Meanwhile large ivory cells slid with aimless dignity from the cobbled openings of Ketut's blood vessels, and tried to absorb the microbes by surrounding and engulfing them. Madai had seen pictures of these white blood cells that kill germs, but the nasty little bugs far outnumbered Ketut's natural protectors. Soon the bacteria would sweep through his body, killing and dividing—and feasting on his rotting flesh.

"What should I do?" Madai asked the Moonbird.

"You'd better kill them before they kill Ketut."

"How do I kill them?"

"How do you kill beetles that get in your rice?"

"I crush them with my fingers," said Madai.

"Perhaps that will work."

"But there are so many of them."

"That's how they kill."

There was no more time for talk. The foul microbes were beginning to swarm up the Moonbird's legs, and were crawling onto Madai's bare feet. The Moonbird plucked them off in great gobs and crushed them with its beak. Madai had no time to waste as they crawled up his legs in itchy, burning clumps. He grabbed clusters with his bare hands and mashed them between his palms like ripe berries, where they left a stinging, gooey mess. But the residue of moon-milk still subtly glowing on his skin protected him from their poisonous sting.

He crushed countless slimy grapelike clusters between his burning palms. The Moonbird scooped them up in masses and destroyed them with its beak. And still there were more—and more. Millions of them clinging to Ketut's flesh, mindlessly killing and feeding and dividing. Trying to fasten onto Madai's bare legs, with only the Moonbird and the aimless white blood cells to help fend them off.

"There's no end to them," gasped Madai, crushing a biting cluster that had formed on his knee. "I need a weapon."

"Did you bring anything with you?"

"Only my flashlight."

"Try it."

Madai discovered that the direct beam of the flashlight generated enough heat to pop the microbes like bubbles. But there were so many of them, and the range and power of his flashlight was so limited.

They mustered all of their might to maneuver inside the gaping wound, crushing the vile clusters, bursting them with the heat of the flashlight beam—and hoping that the army of white blood cells would increase in strength and numbers to combat and absorb the invaders. Madai waded with itchy, burning feet through a slippery mess of rotting flesh and dead microbes.

The task continued endlessly. Madai's mind whirled with fatigue. Still they moved among the besieged muscle fibers, finding the foul creatures and destroying them.

The number of microbes began to diminish—but so did the strength of the flashlight beam, which gradually dimmed, making their task even more difficult in the slimy darkness. Still they worked on, tirelessly slaying their microscopic enemies.

"Look!" said the Moonbird with real surprise.

Madai paused to look around, and in the fluttering beam of light he saw that the tide of battle had turned in their favor. They had decimated the invaders, which were now far outnumbered by the white blood cells—that greedily gobbled up the destroyers like a child gobbles its supper.

Madai felt drained.

"Ketut's own defenses will be able to fight them off now," said the Moonbird. "Let's go."

They rose out of the sleeping boy—who rested quietly now. They lifted over the house and the village, and dived under the muddy Waringan River to wash away the stinging slime.

Madai saw with regret that the cool waters also swirled away the glowing nimbus of protective moon-milk.

At last the Moonbird deposited Madai in a depleted heap in the marshy forest clearing. By the position of the sun, he knew it was already late afternoon. Madai rose up from the forest floor and stumbled back to his compound.

Ketut was now awake, looking pale and bony, with big, sunken eyes. But his fever had broken, his ankle was less swollen, and he was no longer crying with pain. Their gentle older sister, Dawan, patiently spooned warm coco-milk into his parched mouth.

As Madai entered, his mother looked at him oddly and exclaimed, "There you are, strange one! Why have you been gone all day? Your aunt, Menkarma, saw you dozing in the forest, mumbling and dreaming, and you refused to wake up when she hailed you. Your hands and feet look all red and blistered from forest gnat bites. You must be more careful! Why did you go off sleeping in the woods all day? Don't you care that your brother has been sick?"

Madai felt elated, confused—and frightened. If he could heal Ketut, he could cure others. *Must* cure others. But there were so many on the island who needed help. Could he heal them all with just his bare hands and the beam of his flashlight? It was difficult and dangerous work, not pleasant like plucking shellfish from the peaceful and colorful coral reefs.

Madai tried to forget all about it. Perhaps healing Ketut was a fluke. Maybe his brother would have recovered anyway. Perhaps the whole thing was a figment of Madai's imagination. But he couldn't forget it. The memory of entering the cramped, dank interior of his brother's body to mop up the venom and battle the germbugs continued to haunt him—even in his dreams. How could such a thing be possible? What should he do?

Madai didn't try it again for many months. Then their sweet, smiling baby cousin in the next compound developed a bad earache. Madai and his family could hear the infant screaming frantically with pain day and night, and they all knew that if the swelling didn't subside soon the child would grow deaf—or die.

Brahman priests were called in to chant their healing mantras. Itinerant herb-women busily brewed up their soothing concoctions. Nothing helped, and gloom settled over the close-knit desa community.

Madai fretted and worried. Could the Moonbird carry him inside the infant's ear to combat the microbes? Did he *want* to—yet how could he refuse if it were possible? Why were such strange choices thrust upon him? All he'd wanted was to see interesting places and dive for shellfish.

The baby was declining fast. It couldn't hold fluids and was drying up with pain and fever. If Madai was going to act, it had to be *now*.

He went into the forest to summon the Moonbird—armed with his flashlight, pocketknife, rubber thong sandals, and strips of palmleaf, which he could tie around his bare hands for protection.

"Can you take me inside a baby's ear?" he asked when the Garuda appeared.

"I was waiting for you to call me," whispered the Moonbird. "We mustn't delay. We must work fast or the child will shrivel and die before dusk."

It was nasty work. They entered through the baby's screaming mouth, and crawled into a narrow passageway that was clogged with bacteria clusters, dead white blood cells, and rotting tissues. Using his flashlight to see, and working slowly and carefully, Madai used his pocketknife blade to gradually scrape the muck out of the tortuous ear canals, and into the baby's throat to be coughed up. The child thrashed and rolled, making the job even more difficult for Madai, who felt like he was being tossed in the surf. Yet he had to move with utmost precision despite the tumult, otherwise his knife blade would cut into the constricted ear tunnels and cause even more damage.

After hours of this repellent task, the baby's ears were cleared and the child slept peacefully. Again Madai felt excited but bewildered. Why did he have such uncanny powers—and what should he do?

Again he tried to forget about it. Maybe the baby's ears would have healed naturally. But again and again some beloved village face twisted with pain and roused Madai's sympathy—so that he *cared* and had to help.

His aunt's bladder was blocked with stones—it was a simple matter to pluck them out. A fisherman stepped on a broken beer bottle and shards of glass were painfully embedded in his foot. How *easy* it was to remove them. The children in the mission school were complaining and itching with lice. What fun to wander on their scalps, through forests of thick black hair—to stalk the ugly gray lice lurking like multilegged tigers in the jungle, and skewer the scuttling beasts with his pocketknife. Germbugs were harder and more disagreeable work, but his fighting skills gradually increased and Madai felt a greater and greater sense of power.

He spent more of his time entranced in the forest, clutching the moonstone image of the Garuda and mumbling to himself. Fewer of these magical hours were devoted to reef diving and exploring exotic realms—for there was always somebody in the communal desa who needed his help.

And the desa is a small, closely woven community where little can be hidden. Madai's strange sojourns into the forest gradually became known, and people slowly realized that Madai was truly odd—and that he could sometimes help them.

If someone grew ill and Madai went into the forest to sit and dream in his mysterious way, the sick one would often grow swiftly well. Often—but not always.

He couldn't heal everyone. Some died no matter how long he remained entranced. At times he sat dreaming for so long that his skin grew pale or covered with welts, and sweat poured from his compact body until the villagers feared that Madai himself would die.

By the time he was nineteen, islanders often came to Madai with ailing relatives, and asked him to dream in the forest to cure them. Madai wasn't always willing. Sometimes he hid from them or snapped that he couldn't help. But usually he took pity and went off to the banyan grove—and the unfortunate one might recover that same day.

"My daughter is very ill. Please help her, Madai."

"My heart is growing weak and feeble, fluttering like a dying bird. Help me Madai."

"I'm going blind. Help me . . ."

"I have the shaking malaria fever. Help me . . ."

"My mother has terrible pains in her gut. Help her . . ."

"My baby coughs up his milk. He's growing thin and feeble. Help him . . ."

"My skin is covered with sores. Help me . . ."

"My son is burning with measles. Help him . . ."

The news spread rapidly around the island, and even as far as Bali. Soon everyone knew that the island was blessed with a magician who could truly heal the ill.

The Brahman priests had always said healing prayers, and herbalists and the gentle mission nuns dispensed simple medicines and health advice—but there were so many things they could never help.

The Chinese store sold a dusty assortment of pills and ginseng powder, Tiger Balm and other ointments, but they were too expensive for most islanders, and often ineffective after sitting in the equatorial heat. Few villagers could afford the mail boat to the big hospital on Bali—and there were so many things that even the hospital couldn't cure.

There were those who'd claimed to be miracle workers in the past, but none had been very powerful—at least not in the memory of most living islanders. The elders remembered tales from their childhood of a woman who could cut out diseases and evil spirits with her bare hands, but she'd died long ago. Madai was the first genuine healer to appear since legendary times. And his cures often worked.

People began to follow him, begging for help. Soon he was tagged by a ragged band of the feverish, coughing, and lame, and their weeping relatives imploring his aid.

"My brother just broke his back, help him Madai!"

"My wife miscarried and she's bleeding to death. Help her."

"This rash itches like hell. Help me, Madai."

The people began to bring him elaborate gifts and offerings of fruit and fish, rice and tinned foods from the Chinese store. At first he refused the gifts, but his family insisted he take them.

"If he's dreaming in the forest for you, he can't catch any lobsters to help feed the family," explained his mother as she eagerly accepted the sacks of rice and prettily arranged baskets of foods and flowers.

One item that Madai himself always demanded was flashlight batteries. The young healer seemed to have an insatiable desire for batteries, which made him seem even stranger to the islanders.

Madai pored through the books at the mission library, learning all he could about modern medicines, and the causes and cures of disease. He studied with the itinerant herb doctors who wander the island dispensing traditional remedies.

He spoke to the shaven-headed Brahman priests at the village temple, behind the mossy gateways of elaborately carved sandstone. They told him tales of gods that inhabit the mountains and demons that swim in the depths of the seas. They instructed him in the ancient rituals of diagnosis and healing prayers.

Madai learned that there was frequently no need to call on the Moonbird. People who came to him with hope burning in their eyes could often be healed by simpler means, such as the recitation of Vedic prayers, the warming touch of his hands, or the use of simple packaged medicines, soothing herbal teas, and poultices. Madai quickly grew skilled in such arts.

But if the ailment couldn't be treated with prayer and touch, faith and herbs, then he went into the forest to ride the Moonbird, and entered the bodies armed only with his sinewy hands, his knife and flashlight. To battle the disease until he destroyed it.

Sometimes he found life-forms so fierce that he feared for his own life. Not just the monstrous little microbes that swarmed in every nasty shape and color, but creeping gray-green fungi that had to be slashed from the flesh, and horrible wriggling worms that stayed alive even when cut, and had to be smashed with his sandaled feet.

Madai hated to look at such things and hated to touch them, but only by killing the foul creatures could he save lives. Sometimes he couldn't save them no matter how hard he tried. He learned this after several tragic failures that claimed the sufferer's life—and almost claimed his own.

Once they entered an old man who was so choked with the ugly tendrils of a cancerous tumor that there was no room at all for Madai and the Moonbird to move about. They were trapped when the tumor surrounded them, and had to tear desperately at the growth with beak and hands and knife to free themselves. When they finally escaped, they realized there was no way to fight such a monstrous growth of cells, when the body mysteriously devours itself.

Madai learned that if an illness were too far advanced he couldn't cure it, and would risk his own life for nothing. He learned to refuse the tearful pleas of the relatives in such cases, though it made him sad to say no and doom the sick one to certain death.

He also discovered complaints that he could never heal. "Why?" he asked the Moonbird.

"There are many kinds of pain," whispered the patient voice of the shimmering Garuda in his mind. "There is sickness caused by filth—the tiny, nasty bugs that we can destroy if the invasion hasn't progressed too far. There is entropy, when nothing evil grows inside the body, but it is worn with weakness and age. There is no way we can heal such a body. It must be discarded so the soul can float like a butterfly to the mountain in the center of the universe. There is sickness brought by unfortunate karma, disharmony, and demonic curses. Those must be healed with faith and touch and prayer, for there is no sickness in the flesh—only in the mind. There is the pain of bodies which are broken, burned, or torn. They can only be healed with soothing herbs and restful time. There are bodies that devour themselves with tumorous growths. If the growth is small we can destroy it, but if it has already spread, there is nothing we can do. We can only *try* to help the people of your island."

The villagers flocked to Madai's compound daily to beg for healings, and he tried to help them whenever he could. Yet all the while he wondered how he had ever gotten caught in such strangeness, and how long it could last. Would he spend his life soothing other people's tormented flesh—and never enjoy a life of his own?

10

There was one person in the desa who could make Madai laugh. One person who restored rather than sapped his strength—and that was Lasmi. One sultry evening Madai eagerly set out along the pathway to her compound, carrying a dusty box of Dutch chocolates from the Chinese store that was given to him by a man who was grateful to be relieved of boils.

As Madai's renown as a healer grew, Lasmi's attitude toward him changed. They no longer talked of going to big cities together, and she no longer demanded that they marry. She understood that marriage would somehow rob him of the power to heal. Yet she didn't hold him in awe, unlike so many islanders. When he came to her compound, tense and wearied from battling some noxious creature, Lasmi greeted him with gentle affection and playful teasing that brightened his mood, and made him smile as if he were a child again.

The monsoon would soon be upon them, and already the air was heavy with moisture that descended on Madai in a diffuse drizzle from the vine-clad trees. Birds jabbered in the dense foliage, excitedly gossiping about a lush crop of palm nuts as they settled down for the night. Insects chirped mindlessly, and frogs sang their love songs.

As Madai's powers grew, he became ever more aware of the lifebeat of the forest—even without the Moonbird. He stopped for a moment and leaned against the thick aerial root of a banyan, and listened to the polyphonic swirl of sound.

At his back came an airy sigh—the voice of the banyan tree, which speaks very rarely, for it has very little to say.

"*I am olden and slowed and my span has been long. You nestle against me young and quick as the grass. Take pleasure in your newness, for your span is brief and you will lose it soon enough.*" The ancient tree sighed again and fell silent.

The banyan is right, thought Madai. *It understands me better than I understand myself. I won't stay young forever and I don't want to grow old alone. I want to enjoy my life—with Lasmi. I'll persuade the Moonbird that I can marry, yet continue the healings. The Moonbird has said that most things are possible—so let my joy and contentment be possible too!*

Madai felt cheered as he continued along the pathway toward the muddy clearing that held Lasmi's shabby family compound. But when he arrived he found an unpleasant surprise. Another man had come to call on Lasmi: the rich widower Ram.

Madai lurked in the bushes, feeling a sad mist close around him as he watched the distasteful scene. In the earthern clearing before the worn wicker sleeping hut squatted Lasmi, her mother, and the lanky widower Ram, all dressed in holiday sarongs embroidered with gilded thread. The sallow widower made some coarse joke and guffawed, revealing a mouth filled with glittering gold teeth that he'd bought on a visit to Bali.

Lasmi and her mother tittered like sparrows.

Lasmi's mother served small china cups of rice wine, which Ram sucked noisily through his wispy moustache. The widower leered as he watched Lasmi demurely sip her wine. His sharp eyes trailed eagerly down her fine-featured face and thick black hair to her lithe, high-breasted body, draped in a lacy yellow *kebaya* blouse, and a graceful holiday sarong adorned with a pattern of flying golden birds. Lasmi's mother watched with a gap-toothed grin as the wealthy widower, owner of vast orchards and rice terraces, watched her lovely daughter.

Madai dejectedly watched the scene unfold.

Ram had brought gifts—courting gifts, which he presented to Lasmi's mother with ceremonial courtesy. First a bolt of lustrous silk brocade, glowing with a floral pattern of rich purples and blues. Then a sack of white rice. Then a tinned Australian ham, matches, and brown laundry soap from the Chinese store. Then a set of silver bangles—gold would come later if they were wed. Then a bolt of good cotton batik for everyday sarongs for Lasmi, her mother, and sister. Then rubber thong sandals for the entire family. Then tins of soy sauce and sweet condensed milk. Then a basket of ripe, pungent durian fruit, prettily arranged on a bed of ferns by one of Ram's servants.

As the pile of gifts on the neatly swept earthern floor of the compound increased, Lasmi's mother's smile widened, and so did the widower Ram's. Lasmi gazed at the gifts with serene disinterest while Madai hunched miserably in the concealing shrubs and watched with clouded eyes.

He'd looked forward to their meeting all day. He longed for soft caresses and whispered, silly talk. If Lasmi moved into Ram's house, became his wife, and bore his children, there'd be nobody for him on the island at all. No other woman had ever interested him. Ever since he was a child, there was only one girl that he liked to talk and play with, one who shared his interest in books, and one girl that he yearned for—Lasmi.

Now he had lost her. Why? So he could continue healing the sick ones. So he could help other people. What about Madai? How could he cure others if his own heart was sick and sore? Would he ever live like a normal man, or must he be like the mission priest, always caring for others instead of himself? Was the power to ride the Moonbird a blessing or a curse?

Perhaps he should talk to Lasmi after Ram left, and persuade her to lie with him that night. Perhaps he should forget about the shimmering bird of his boyhood, and the crying, pleading ones, and become a grown man now, fishing and fathering a family that would become the center of his life. Why must he always be the strange one, the odd one, the one who must wait?

Yet how could he give up the precious Moonbird? The afflicted ones needed him so badly. Ketut would have died without his powers, and so would many others. How could he renounce that?

Ram looked so smug, displaying his glittering teeth like a proud old rooster, and dazzling Lasmi's mother with rich gifts. How could that old man believe that Lasmi loved him? His devious plan was clear: he would win the heart of her impoverished mother, who would pressure her daughter into marriage. How could her needy mother resist Ram's ostentatious wealth, and how could Lasmi resist her poor mother's pleas that she marry into a powerful family that could provide all their needs? Her mother would scoff if Lasmi said she wanted to wait for Madai, the strange one.

Ram knew that his courting gifts wouldn't be refused, and Ram was sly. He was renowned on the island as a mean and heartless landlord. Since he had no heart of his own, he didn't need Lasmi's heart—her body would suffice. Only Madai cared about Lasmi's feelings, and he had no wealth to offer—only his warmth.

He hated Ram for toying with their need. The rich widower looked so smug as Madai stared at him with fiery wrath.

There was a sudden rustling in the bushes, and something moved with a bluish, phosphorescent glow. Then from the brush a white tusked face lifted out of a tangle of long, coppery hair. A trembling, clawed hand beckoned. Cold eyes stared at him and an icy smile flickered briefly across the sneering lips.

Madai wanted to cry out, but as in dreams, no sound would come. He stared at the hideous face with terrified surprise.

"What do *you* want, Rangda?" he managed to say.

The flickering face laughed mirthlessly. "Shall we *see* him, my son?" hissed the hoarse voice in his mind.

"No!"

"When you learn to see as Rangda sees, your powers will grow as vast as the seas."

"I don't want more power. Leave me alone!"

The bluish, phosphorescent glow surrounded the widower Ram like a terrible dream, and his form began to shift and change. His skin acquired a pasty, yellowish tone. Then gradually his flesh began to crack and peel like a tourist who has fallen asleep in the equatorial sun. But there was no red color of sunburn, only a jaundiced yellow.

Ram continued to sip his rice wine and eye Lasmi as the skin cracked and peeled from his face, from his spindly arms and legs, from his sunken, hairless chest and curved back. Ram seemed to notice nothing, though his skin peeled off in long, shriveled strips, and the dreamlike phosphorescent blue surrounded him.

Now the flesh underneath the skin began to slowly dissolve into bloody tendrils that slipped away from Ram's bones. The flesh of his face began to slide away, revealing the underlying cartilage and flashing golden teeth. The flesh of Ram's neck oozed away, exposing large, throbbing veins and delicate ligaments. The flesh of his torso dripped to the earthern floor of the compound. Still he drank his wine and joked with Lasmi's mother.

Now Madai could see Ram's ribs and his beating heart, and the guts inside his abdomen. The long, sinewy muscles of Ram's arms and legs hung from his stringy limbs. Finally the inner organs began to decompose, and Ram's eyes clouded over.

"*See*, my son," hissed the hoarse voice inside Madai's mind. "If you learn to see, no one can ever cause you sorrow."

"No!" whispered Madai, trapped in this horrible waking dream. "I don't want to *see*—I'm *not* your son! Go away!"

The big white clip-tailed ape watched with worried black eyes from the treetops, then shrieked and dashed away.

11

The nightmare vision lingered with Madai all the next day. He felt a sense of dread in his gut that wouldn't go away. He didn't go to the mission library or the temple, or even diving for shellfish, telling his mother that he felt tired. He sat listlessly around the humid family compound, ignoring the sick ones, brushing away spiteful flies, and helping his mother strip bamboo to make baskets. Until a surge of anxiety finally drove him to Lasmi's worn wicker compound at the muddy seaward side of the desa.

"Will you marry Ram?" he demanded when he found her making coco-milk.

"I don't know," she said, with uncertain dark eyes.

But Lasmi was spared the painful decision, for word soon filtered around the communal desa that Ram was seriously ill. Madai's tension grew in the next month as Ram's health gradually declined. Soon the entire village knew that the widower was dying of a large cancerous tumor in his belly. He went to the big hospital on Bali by the weekly mail boat, accompanied by a retinue of servants. But the doctors sent him home, saying it was too late to operate, and he couldn't be cured.

When Madai heard the news he shivered with rage. He ran to the big temple at the edge of the village late that moonlit night. He marched between the huge carved gateways of mossy, crumbling sandstone, and crept inside the thatched, seven-tiered pagoda in the center of the complex, which represents the mountain in the center of the universe. On the altar to Siva the Destroyer was a small wicker hut that held the image of Rangda the Antagonist.

"Come here, Rangda!" he demanded. "I want to talk to you."

Nothing happened. There was silence except for the babble of courting frogs and the buzzing of fragile night insects.

"Don't hide. I know you're lurking in here somewhere."

Silence.

"I won't leave until you appear. I must ask you something."

Silence.

"*Rangda!*"
The image on the altar stirred slightly—or was it just his imagination? It began to flicker with a blue glow.
"Rangda, come here!"
The white tusked face with the long, draping tangle of copper hair glowed icy blue. The bulging black eyes stared at him coldly. The mouth sneered, and a clawed left hand trembled.
"Rangda," demanded Madai. "Why did you cause Ram's illness?"
"I didn't *cause,*" hissed a hoarse voice in his mind. "I simply asked you to *see.*"
"Wherever you look, something horrible happens."
"Most things happen—whether I see them or not."
"Why did you decide to see Ram dissolving?"
"Was it me who decided—or *you?*" smiled Rangda. "I ask you to see. You decide where to cast your eyes."
"That's a *lie!*"
"Not lies. I have no quarrels with Ram," said Rangda. "He's generous with his puja offerings. *You* have quarrels with Ram; isn't it so?"
"That's not true."
"That *is* true."
"You're the one who caused him to get sick," insisted Madai.
"I cause nothing. I simply see. Perhaps *you* caused it."
"*I can't cause disease!*"
"You make folks so well. Perhaps now you also make them sick," laughed Rangda.
"You *forced* me to look."
"I asked you to *see.* You decided who to see and what to cause."
"How?"
"Perhaps you were so angry with Ram."
"I would *never* cause disease, even if I were angry."
"If you could cause sickness, you'd be so strong," cackled Rangda.
"I don't want that kind of awful power! I don't want any power. I want to live like everyone else on the island."
"Sailing with the fishermen and breeding like the chickens?"
"Yes, maybe it's time for me to live like that," said Madai. "It would make Lasmi happy, and our families too. It was fun flying around the island on the Moonbird and diving in the reef for lobsters. I wanted it to go on and on. I thought we could fly away from the island to see wonderful things. Then I had to kill those nasty bugs that grew inside Ketut, or he would have died. Soon everyone

was asking me to heal them. I don't mind. I'm not a doctor, but I like to help. Now you tell me to *see*—and if I'm angry someone will weaken and die! I don't want such weird powers. It's time to load myself with adult burdens and grow too heavy to ride the Moonbird —or to see your ugly face. It's time to stop this and live like an ordinary man."

"We'll see," smiled Rangda.

"What pleasure do you get from your *seeing?*" demanded Madai. "I think you suck at life like a vampire."

"I don't suck blood like some coarse bat spirit," hissed Rangda, clearly offended.

"Then how do you live, witch? You don't take food or drink with the islanders. How have you survived so many miserable years?"

"Sipping *vitality*. You can learn to sip it too. The banyan says your span is brief, but it needn't be so. Your span can be boundless if you sup with me—my son."

"So, you confess that when you *see*, you drain vitality to preserve your own loathsome life—and your victim sickens and dies."

"I confess nothing, I simply see," said Rangda. Then the tusked, phosphorescent face sank back into its tangle of coppery hair and was still.

Madai stomped angrily out of the central pagoda and the carved sandstone gateways, and back to his sleeping mat, where he tossed fitfully until morning.

Was it possible that Rangda spoke the truth? Was it possible that Madai's jealous anger *caused* Ram's disease?

The next day Ram's relatives were at Madai's wicker gate laden with elaborate gifts of rice and eggs, chickens and fruit, and bolts of batik cloth from the Chinese store. Ram's health was steadily declining. They begged Madai to sit entranced and dream in the forest to heal him.

At first Madai refused. It was Rangda's fault; let Rangda cure him. Yet if he were somehow to blame for Ram's illness, a healing would be the only way to end his feelings of doubt and shame. Madai decided to try one more cure, of the widower Ram. Then he would put an end to all of this and marry Lasmi—and get on with his own life.

His mother and Dawan graciously accepted the generous gifts from Ram's relatives. Then Madai tucked a flashlight and his sharpened pocketknife into his pouch, and trudged sullenly into the forest, to the marshy clearing among the groves of banyans and bamboos.

Why did it have to be a tumor? That was so difficult and dangerous to destroy. He'd already explained to Ram's family that if the growth were too advanced, he could do nothing. But they pleaded with him with faithful eyes to do his best. Now he must risk his own life—to heal his rival.

Madai took the tiny, roughly carved moonstone image of the Garuda, servant of Visnu the Preserver, from a filigreed silver amulet around his neck. He held it up to the intense equatorial sunlight and gazed at the inner luminescence of the stone. As always, this had a hypnotic effect. Soon his muscles relaxed and his lips parted, his breathing grew deep and regular, his eyes focused on the image, and his mind grew calm, clear, and peacefully afloat.

Usually the Moonbird appeared at once. Yet Madai sat and stared into the image until his eyes burned—and nothing happened.

"Moonbird," he called. "Where are you?"

For a long time there was only silence broken by the drone of insects, the calling of village roosters, and the gossipy chatter of birds.

Finally there came the familiar rustle of wings. His eyes closed, and when they opened, the shimmering Garuda stood before him.

"Where were you?" frowned Madai.

"Your mind is cloudy today," whispered the Moonbird. "It was difficult to find you."

"I'm worried about the widower Ram. He has a big tumor in his belly. His relatives want me to heal him."

"You've done that before. Why are you so frightened?"

"Because Rangda showed me his body decaying, and the witch insists that I *caused* Ram's illness because I was jealous and angry."

"If the growth isn't too large we'll try to destroy it—if you *want* to heal Ram," whispered Moonbird.

"Of course I want to heal him!" snapped Madai. "Why would I want him to die? Are you also accusing me of making him ill? It was *Rangda*, not I!"

"Your mind is so cloudy today, it's hard to know what you want."

"I said I *want* to—"

"Then climb on my back and bring your sharpest knife."

Madai clambered onto the silky back of the Moonbird, but the eagle-god didn't move; it stood there silently.

"What's wrong?" asked Madai.

"I don't know," said Moonbird. "You feel dense and heavy today. It will be difficult to carry you."

"Why?"

"Perhaps you're too apprehensive. We should gather some moon-milk to protect you."

"No," said Madai, stiff with pride. "There's no time to fight the moon demons. If I've caused Ram's illness, then I'll heal him—without any protection."

The big Garuda looked at him quizzically, then tensed its muscles and rose above the thick green forest. They moved slowly over the tangled treetops to the desa. They circled Ram's peaked thatch and ebony sleeping house and entered the spacious and elaborate dwelling, which reeked of disease.

Time and space folded into itself . . .

12

Ram lay curled listlessly on his ornately carved sleeping platform, with a stained sarong tucked loosely around his sunken waist. Madai hadn't seen Ram since the horrible vision, and he was shocked at how skeletal the widower had become. His stringy hair and thin beard hung in sweaty wisps around his gaunt, vacant-eyed face. His bones showed clearly beneath dry, sallow skin. He stared blankly ahead, and his painful breathing was labored and shallow.

"It may be too late to save him," murmured Madai.

"Do you want to go inside?" asked the Moonbird.

"I want to try."

The inside of Ram's body was like a jungle run amuck. Instead of the neat and orderly array of body cavities filled with plump organs, tubes, and living structures, a wild, vinelike growth had multiplied crazily and invaded everywhere.

The tendrils of rapidly growing tumor sprouted from somewhere deep inside his intestines. By now they had entered every crevice of Ram's abdomen. Exuding droplets of strong acid, the exploring fingers of cancerous tissue had insinuated themselves into Ram's inner organs.

Tendrils of the vinelike growth were breaking and floating off to sprout everywhere. There was a sharp, acid odor as the wildly dividing tumor cells probed, dissolved, and invaded the remaining healthy flesh.

"I think we're too late," whispered the Moonbird.

"No," insisted Madai. "We'll fight it. No one will ever say that I was too jealous to heal Ram."

"But it's already spread all over his body."

"Then we'll attack it all over his body." Madai jumped off the Moonbird, pulled his small, sharp knife from his pouch, and slashed at the vinelike growths, carefully avoiding cutting any healthy pink tissue. But as he hacked the grayish pieces away, they merely floated off and reestablished themselves—and began sprouting elsewhere.

Furiously Madai cut and slashed at the cancerous tendrils—that began to curl and lash at his own bare legs with their burning acids. It seemed hopeless. He cut and hacked with all his strength, and the severed bits merely floated away and began to grow again.

One long, whiplike tendril fastened onto his thigh and began to bore into his skin. The Moonbird's beak deftly tore it from Madai's leg, where it left a painful wound. Another piece fastened to Madai's back and the Moonbird ripped it away.

"What should we do?" gasped Madai. "I can't kill it by cutting—it just keeps sprouting and growing. I've never seen anything grow so fast!"

"How do you kill the weeds that clog the orchards and vegetable gardens?" asked the Moonbird.

"We cut and burn them," said Madai. "Yes, *burning* would destroy the growth—but how do I create a fire without burning Ram?"

A fat tumor finger probed at his neck. With a yelp of pain, Madai tore it away.

"It can't be destroyed with your hands or knife. If you cannot burn it away, Ram will soon be dead," said the Moonbird.

"The tumor secretes little bubbles of acid *outside* its cell walls," said Madai. "If we could get the acid *inside* the tumor cells, they might dissolve themselves. Let me try."

Madai made a rough, jagged cut through one tumor finger and skewered it with his knife. He rubbed the open, cut edge against the bubbles of acid—and the severed finger withered with a sputtering sound.

"It works!" shouted Madai. "But it'll take forever to cut open each piece with this little knife, and rub it against the acid until it melts."

"Then we should leave," said the Moonbird. "Perhaps the growth is too far advanced for us to combat."

"No. We'll stay."

They worked swiftly, cutting each tendril into segments, skewering them on the knife or on the Moonbird's long, sharp beak, and dissolving them in the cancer's own acid.

But as they fought, the nodules weren't quiescent. The undissolved pieces continued to grow and flourish, multiply and divide, separate and take root, sprout and grow and multiply and divide . . . The segments fastened onto Ram's organs and invaded the flesh as they grew crazily. The greedy fragments tried to establish themselves on Madai too. They had to be torn away, until his skin was covered with burning sores.

They cut, skewered, and dissolved them as fast as they could, but the tendrils divided and sprouted with wild speed. Wearily Madai wondered whether he could move faster than the growth, and whether his strength would hold out.

They cut and skewered and dissolved . . . Cut, skewered, and dissolved . . . Still the tumor spread and flourished as they cut it into jagged pieces, and melted it in its own acids.

"It may overwhelm us," said the Moonbird. "We should leave while you still have the strength to move—and let Ram die."

"We'll stay," insisted Madai, shaky with exhaustion as the sweat beaded his feverish skin.

He wrenched off a large, flapping segment that fastened onto his head and burrowed rapidly into his scalp, with a burning pain that made him weep.

And they cut, skewered, dissolved . . . Cut, skewered, dissolved . . .

The villagers were worried. Madai had been sitting entranced in the forest for two days, trying to heal Ram. His eyes were tightly closed. His limbs shook as he muttered to himself. His face was ashen and gaunt, and sweat poured down his slight body. Worst of all, strange wounds were appearing all over his skin and scalp, and his hair was falling out in tufts.

"Let's wake him up," growled his father. "Or Ram's sickness will kill Madai!"

Though they shook him and yelled directly into his face, nothing could wake him. The shaven-headed temple priests came to see Madai, and suggested that he was possessed by Rangda the Antagonist. They chanted puja on his behalf. Father Hans, the missionary priest, thought he might be possessed by a devil, and said a special mass. Lasmi, Dawan, and their mothers came—and wept.

Cut, skewer, dissolve . . . Cut, skewer, dissolve . . . with limbs that were too tired to move. The Moonbird insisted they leave before Madai collapsed in the toxic acids. He stubbornly refused. He would kill the cancer that was killing Ram as *proof* that this wasn't his fault.

Cut, skewer, dissolve . . . At last they made some headway against the lethal growth.

On the third morning Madai awoke. So did the widower Ram, who said he felt stronger and ate a little rice gruel.

Madai fell back into a stupor and was carried home. His limbs were weak and the sores were painful, and the hair continued to fall from his blistered head. They laid him on his sleeping mat, and his mother and Dawan washed him and spooned coco-water while Ram's relatives heaped more gifts at his poor feet.

The villagers were awed. In the afternoon Ram was strong enough to get up and take a short stroll around his spacious, shady compound.

Madai sank into a deep, comatose sleep.

In Madai's sleep there was nothing except vast darkness and silence. Then the Moonbird appeared in shimmering moonstone light.

"Shall I die now?" asked Madai.

"Do you want to die?" whispered the Moonbird.

"It's very still and peaceful here, like the calm depths of the sea. Why should I return to the churning confusion of the desa?"

"Would you like to stay in this place forever?" asked the Moonbird.

"I'd miss Lasmi though, and my family."

"You must recover your strength."

"It's hard to stay strong with the sick ones following me. If I lost my strength they'd leave me alone—perhaps it would be better that way."

"Shall I take you to a peaceful undersea realm where you can rest?"

"What sort of place is it?" asked Madai, feeling a tiny twinge of curiosity rising out of his diffuse numbness.

"The Naga Queen is very grateful to us for rescuing her and the blind prince from Basudara's funeral pyre. She and her son have safely returned to her father's kingdom in the deepest silence of the sea. She will welcome you gladly. You can dream there and recover."

"I'd like to see the Naga Queen's kingdom," said Madai.

Mahanagini dwelled in a resplendent palace of intricately carved golden coral, studded with shells and pearls. Madai clung weakly to the silken back of the Moonbird as they descended through the shadows of the sea and entered the translucent gates of the palace.

They found the Naga Queen resting upon her coiled dragon tail, cradling the blind prince in her arms. The glimmering halo of cobra hoods that surrounded her handsome face expanded with surprise when they glided to the foot of her mother-of-pearl throne. Her slit eyes opened widely and she bowed in cordial greeting.

"The man-child has been weakened in battle," said the Moonbird. "He needs a quiet place to rest and his strength must be restored."

"Kaliya guards the renewing water, and he doesn't part with it gladly," said the Naga Queen. "I will go with you to his grotto, to persuade him to share some with the lad." The Queen slithered off her throne and gently handed her sightless child to an attendant.

They glided together to the underwater den of the great Naga-dragon Kaliya, whose noxious breath scorches the fish who swim past his gateway. The Naga Queen slapped at the water with her hands to announce their arrival.

Kaliya appeared, belching fire. His eyes were red and angry, and his hoods were puffed with venom. Behind him was a retinue of red-scaled Naga warriors with drawn kris daggers. Naga maidservants peeked from the courtyard, adorned with sparkling pearls.

"I must have some renewing water for this boy," said Mahanagini.

"The sacred water is not for earthkind," snorted Kaliya, releasing clouds of foul fumes.

"This boy is companion of the Garuda who saved me from my husband's funeral pyre. I owe them a gift from my father's realm."

"Then lie with me tonight and create tidal waves." Kaliya winked gravely.

"I will *never* lie with you," said the Naga Queen.

"Then I will not part with the renewing water."

Moving with a quick flash of silver-green scales, Mahanagini uncoiled her great, sinuous tail, undulated forward, and struck with lightning fangs that deftly plucked the pearl of immortality from the cleft between Kaliya's eyes.

The monster bellowed with rage and pain, lashed his immense tail, lunged at her with glistening teeth bared—then fell back fearfully. "Give me back my pearl or I will *perish!*"

"Then give us two drops of the sacred water for the man-child, or I will drop the pearl into the void."

Grumbling with anger, Kaliya bared his long, curved fangs, which exuded two clear tears of venom. The Naga Queen collected the droplets in a tiny seashell, then restored Kaliya's vital pearl. The dragon and his entourage sullenly retreated to their smoky den.

The Naga Queen lifted the seashell to Madai's lips and he gingerly sipped the venom. To his surprise, it tasted sweet and refreshing, like salty coco-water.

They returned to the stately Naga-palace, where Mahanagini enveloped Madai's body with her silky serpent coils and shaded his head with her cobra hood. Madai felt a great wave of fatigue and drifted into a languorous sleep, sheltered by the Naga Queen.

He slept there for a long, long while.

Madai finally awoke and found Lasmi kneeling beside his mat, tending his wounds with cool, soothing herbal poultices. The still heat of late afternoon enclosed them, and muted the chirping of geckos and insects, boasting roosters, and family noises from the courtyard. Outside the gate, the villagers and sick ones waited patiently, chanting prayers for Madai's recovery.

Lasmi smiled gently when she saw his eyes open. "You healed Ram and it almost killed you," she said. "Your beautiful black hair is all gone. I love you, Madai. I know you did it for me."

"I did it for Ram," snapped Madai weakly. "He was very ill. Do you think I'm so jealous of your sweetheart that I *want* him to die? Go to him now and be happy."

"No," she said. "I want to stay with you. I understand now that you really have the power to save many lives—it isn't just a crazy new idea from your books. If you marry and lose your power the people will die. Your shiny bald head makes you look like a temple priest, so I'll become like a nun. I've apprenticed myself to an herb doctor to learn poultices and medicinal teas. I'll help you care for the unfortunates and we'll be together always—if you still want to be with me." Their eyes held each other.

"Of course I want it," said Madai. "But now I'm so weak and I look so ugly with this bald head."

"I don't care," smiled Lasmi. "We'll heal the sick ones together. I went gathering herbs and mushrooms early this morning to brew this poultice for your wounds—to heal the healer. Do you like it?" She brushed his cheek with her cool, smooth hand.

"I like it very much," said Madai, with a smile that faded to a frown. "But I wonder if I still have the strength to heal."

III

Strangers came to the island . . .

13

The weekly mail boat was sailing in from Bali, and the rickety wooden dock thronged with noise, color, and crowded confusion. The mail boat was most islanders' only link with the outside world. It delivered kerosene, tinned foods and other supplies, mail, directives from the shadowy central government—and sometimes tourists—with money to spend.

All morning the vendors had busily prepared their wooden stands, selling spicy snacks, sweet fruit juices, and handmade trinkets. Village dance troupes rehearsed their impromptu performances. Bands of barefoot children scampered and smiled winsomely, striking dance poses and dreaming of coins and gum. Young men dressed in their prized T-shirts and foreign jeans to practice their English and guide the tourists for ballpoint pens and other tips. Now the sluggish little boat grew in the distance, and excitement washed over the crowd on the weather-beaten dock.

Ketut waited with the boisterous youths who played card games and bet clove-scented Kratek cigarettes. He wore tight, faded, too short jeans, and a Balinese T-shirt with a Barong's head. Ketut still walked with a limp from the viper's bite, but he was energetic and bright-eyed as always. He was quick with languages, like his brother, Madai, and eager to guide the hardy tourists who trickled from the lavish resorts of Bali to this isolated island.

The foreigners came searching for the archetypal tropical dream. There were no fancy hotels or restaurants here. The only facilities were a simple government lodging house, or rooms at the mission or behind the Chinese store, where a cot and a meal could be bought for a few *rupiah*. Trance dances weren't staged at hotels for tour groups. Here the ancient dances were woven at the temples—for the gods. The people were gentle and spontaneously interested and friendly. The beaches and scenery were postcard splendid, with misted jutting hills clothed in myriad shades of green. The few tourists were welcomed, and often found their dream paradise.

They explored the desas, and the peaked thatch and wicker compounds. They played on the isolated, powdery beaches, lined with nodding coco-palms. They swam and snorkeled among the rainbow coral reefs in the frothy lapis sea. They trekked through orchards and banyan groves, to terraced rice paddies on the hillsides, and even to the crest of Mount Alāka, the glowering volcano in the misty, sparsely inhabited center of the island, where shy aboriginal tribes and leyak spirits dwell.

They waved to the naked brown children playing among the green algae and pastel lotuses in the irrigation ponds, and they gave out chewy rice candy. They watched the skinny dogs, scruffy pigs and chickens scavenging along the muddy alleys of the desas. They snapped countless photos of the ancient sandstone temples adorned with mythical carvings, and the strange ceremonies and shadow puppet dramas. They savored the sweet tropical fruits and the creamy scented flowers. They eyed the pretty young women with bright batik sarongs tucked around their graceful waists.

The realists alertly noted problems of sanitation and poverty. The sportsmen smoked clove-scented krateks, and cheered with the village men at bloody cockfights. And they had *money* to spend.

The sturdy little boat finally docked. The crew began to unload freight, and the passengers swayed down the gangplank: a pair of government officials in stern khaki uniforms, high-caste islanders and a Chinese merchant returning from shopping sprees in Bali, and a few foreigners who were rangy and sunburned, carrying luggage or backpacks, and expensive Japanese cameras. They looked around curiously.

A great clamor rose from the shore. "Sweet perfumed garlands . . . delicious coco-cakes, mangoes and papayas, grilled pork with peanut sauce, ripe passion fruit and mangosteens, spicy fried noodles, beautiful handmade batiks, wood and bone temple carvings, moonstone jewelry, cold lemonade and hot Java coffee, batiks . . . fruit . . . rice cakes . . . carvings . . . scented garlands . . ."

The tourists seemed bewildered by this onslaught, and a bit queasy from their boat ride across the channel from Bali.

"On the road to Mandalay, where the flying fishes play . . ." sang a cheery American. His peeling sunburn and carroty hair and moustache were conspicuous in the jet-haired crowd. He was in his mid-thirties, and wore frayed, cut-off jeans, a flowery shirt, and thong sandals.

"It's beautiful here, Ernie," said a handsome woman in a Balinese batik sundress. Her thick black hair was lightly streaked with silver, and pulled into a loose ponytail. A faint scar ran along one cheek from a childhood fall. She looked around with open delight. "The air is bright and clear and the colors are so intense. The people move so gracefully, carrying baskets on their heads. It's less stylized and simpler than Bali."

"I hope the government guesthouse isn't *too* simple," remarked a pudgy, blond-bearded man with a New Zealand accent, who wore khaki slacks and a safari shirt.

"Come on, Paul!" burbled the russet-haired American. "Where's your sense of adventure? We're like Bob Hope and Bing Crosby and Dorothy Lamour on the road to . . . What's the name of this island again? We've been to so many little islands that I can't keep track of them all. But it's pretty here. Hey, what's that in the palm trees? *Monkeys!* Look at that big white one . . ." Sunburned Ernie began to jump around, making rowdy monkey noises, and plucking imaginary lice from his armpits. His two companions, and Ketut and the other islanders at the salt-scented dock, laughed at his clowning.

"Making a spectacle of yourself, as usual," chuckled Paul. "Come on, we're supposed to be slogging through the leech-infested jungles of Asia, trying to find a genuine healer."

"The shaman on this island is rumored to be very powerful. The Balinese insist he can cure cancer," said the woman, pausing to accept a sweet frangipani flower from a band of tittering, wide-eyed little girls.

"They *all* claim to cure cancer, Sonia," said the bearded New Zealander. "And they all become greedy and commercialized before we ever reach them."

Sonia nodded and tucked the creamy flower in her silvered black hair. The little girls shrieked and scampered away. "We've been tromping from the Philippines to India to Bali, to this tiny island that isn't on most maps, talking to healers, trying to find a miracle worker who can cure poor Jana's lungs."

"Jana is financing our research, and she's paying for my winter sabbatical in the beautiful tropics, so I'll cheerfully do my job," said Paul. "I'll go to every godforsaken island—especially if it has a good beach. I'll interview every half-baked witch doctor, and I'll privately hope that somewhere we'll find one who really has the power. Because I like that bitch Jana Davids, and I don't want her to die of cancer. And because I've always wanted to see a genuine miracle."

"Sonia is a psychologist and I'm a simple physician," said Ernie, no longer clowning. "You're the expert on native cults, Paul. I've seen patients miraculously pull themselves from the edge of death—haven't you *ever* seen a miracle?"

"Not one," said Paul flatly. "I've done anthropological research on native shamans for years. I've never seen a healing that couldn't be attributed to natural causes or coincidence, suggestion or just plain fraud."

"That makes it seem pretty hopeless," said Sonia.

"No, just challenging," said Paul. "Miracles are rare by definition. If they were commonplace, they wouldn't be called miracles. I hope to find one eventually. Maybe today on this humid little island. One is all that I need to make the whole damn search worthwhile."

"I see something worthwhile right in front of us," interrupted Ernie. *"Food stands!"* He grabbed his wife Sonia's hand and pulled her to the smoky row of vendors. He ebulliently gestured and bargained, trading handfuls of coins for grilled skewers of crisp pork with spicy peanut sauce, and banana leaves heaped with fragrant fried noodles, shrimp, and slivered vegetables; hard-boiled eggs in savory tamarind and chili sauce, sweet coconut cakes, rich coffee, and fresh fruit.

He stood near the dock, happily munching and feeding tidbits to Sonia, talking enthusiastically and gesturing at Paul to join them. His broad, sunburned hands precariously balanced plates and cups and skewers, coins and cakes and fruit. The vendors giggled, and Paul watched him with an indulgent smile.

From the fluttering palms, a large white, clip-tailed monkey and his troupe eyed them with bright curiosity, then cavorted among the treetops and raced back into the forest.

A reedy youth with a slight limp approached Paul. "Guide? You need English-speaking guide?"

"We're looking for the healer," said Paul. "Do you know where he is?"

"He's my brother," grinned Ketut. "I will take you to my house. But he cannot help you; he is very weak." The grin faded.

He led the three foreigners, Paul, Sonia, and Ernie, away from the sagging dock, past the rustic government compound, and the mission with its jackwood cross, and the Chinese store with its whirring gas generator; down a winding dirt pathway near the Waringan River, lined with coco-palms, banana trees, and bright flowering shrubs. It was a long walk, sloping uphill in the intense equatorial sun, and the tourists mopped sweat from their flushed faces.

"You want me to buy cold drinks from the Chinese store?" asked Ketut, hoping for a prized, frosty cola.

"No, we have canteens," said Sonia, patting a tepid water bottle at her waist.

"It's beastly hot here, and full of mosquitoes," grumbled Paul. "We've hit the sticky season, which makes it feel hotter and brings out the bugs."

"It's so unspoiled though," said Sonia. "Look at those red flower stalks peeking from the jungle. The village we passed is built in the authentic old style, with ornate ancestral temples, meeting pavilions, and thatched, stilted compounds. I read that the villagers trade their fruit and fish and rice in a communal, extended-family system, so there's no deep poverty—though it's *quite* primitive." She sipped from her canteen, and wished it were a chilled mineral water.

"There weren't beggars at the dock, and everyone looks handsome and healthy," agreed Paul, wiping the sweat from his blond beard, and wanting a bitter-beer. "But there's no electricity, the water supply is the river and irrigation ponds where they wash their clothes and bathe—and they probably drink that same dirty water. I bet all your tropical ailments are here, even if it looks like a postcard."

Ketut waited patiently while the tourists rested in the shade of a great mango tree, drank metallic water from their canteens, and discussed his island. He had learned some facts to explain his home to tourists, and now he spoke up in a bold singsong, as if he were reciting a difficult memorized lesson at school.

"We are a small place with an active volcano, Mount Alāka, in the center. My island was settled long ago by Brahmans fleeing a clan dispute in Bali. Our beliefs are like the Hindu customs of Bali that came from Indian traders centuries ago, but we have developed our own traditions over the years. Our people mostly live in communal desa villages along the Waringan River. We fish and farm, grow rice and fruit, and export some copra, carvings and moonstones. Some simple tribes live by hunting in the remote mountain valleys, but they don't follow our religion or ways . . .

"Because we are so small and isolated, the invaders who swept through this region have largely ignored us; the Muslims and Dutch, the Japanese and tourists. Even the Java government leaves us mostly alone. We live here as our people have lived forever, except for some modern things like outboard motors and kerosene lamps. Someday I'd like to own a transistor radio." Ketut eyed Ernie's bulging backpack and flashed a hopeful smile.

"After we talk to my brother, I can show you an old and beautiful temple in my village. We can sail upriver in my father's boat to view the volcano, though its peak is often bathed in mist. Or we can sail out to the coral reef for snorkeling. I am your guide, so please tell me what you like to do."

"Your English is great," said Sonia.

"I studied at the mission school," smiled Ketut. "It was built long ago when the Dutch were in Indonesia, and it remains to teach the children."

"So you are Christians?" asked Paul.

"Oh no, only Father Hans and the nuns are Christians. We are mostly Hindus on this island, and some Muslims, and the monkey-eating forest people—and the Chinese who run the store."

Ketut was interrupted by the melodious song of flutes and the rhythmic pounding of drums. Then a small procession came into view along the rutted pathway, followed by capering children, bony dogs, and wandering vendors. The men were dressed in their best batik sarongs and gilded headbands. The women wore fragrant flowers twined in their coiled black hair, lacy pastel *kebaya* blouses, brocade sarongs, and silver-and-moonstone amulets around their necks.

They chanted sonorously as they marched slowly along the pathway, carrying a portable altar, which held elaborately arranged offerings of food and flowers, and a large wicker basket shaded with a white silk umbrella and long white banners.

"What's that?" asked Sonia, her flushed face lighting with interest. "I hear music and see intricate patterns everywhere on this island."

"They carry Rangda to their village to ask protection," said Ketut.

"What is *Rangda?*" asked red-haired, red-faced Ernie.

"Rangda is a very bad witch," said Ketut.

"Sounds like my ex-wife," said the pudgy, freckled New Zealander, Paul.

It took them a couple of hours to reach the desa, though even lame Ketut could scamper up the pathway in half that time. He led them to his family compound, where a small band of sick ones squatted in the dense afternoon heat in the muddy clearing, chanting prayers for Madai's recovery from the ordeal of healing Ram.

"This looks promising," murmured Paul. "Are they all waiting for the healer? Why are they singing?"

"They are holding puja and praying that my brother will regain his strength," said Ketut, leading them inside the wicker gateway to the bustling earthern courtyard, rich with the sights, scents, and sounds of rural desa life, then up the narrow ladder of the stilted, rattan sleeping house.

In the filtered light they saw Madai, a sarong tucked loosely around his gaunt waist, languidly brushing away persistent mosquitoes and flies.

"Odd-looking fellow," said Paul. "Looks like he ought to be in hospital himself, he's so frail. Look at that bald head and those big eyes—so dark and sunken and luminous. This *could* be interesting."

14

"Are you Madai the Healer?" asked Paul in a pidgin dialect of Balinese.

"Yes, I am Madai," replied the frail man in accented but perfectly clear English.

"You speak English?"

"A little."

"I'm Dr. Paul Robbes," said the pudgy New Zealander. "I'm professor of anthropology at the University of California. My sunburned friend is Dr. Ernest Spiegle, a doctor who studies unusual medicines. His wife, Sonia, is a psychologist who studies the mind. Pleased to meet you—we've heard lots about you."

"Have you heard that I lost my powers?" frowned Madai.

"What happened?" asked Sonia.

"I battled a powerful enemy—and it made me weak."

"Did you destroy it?" asked Paul.

"Yes, but it was very difficult . . . We went inside Ram's body to fight the growth. The best way to kill a tumor is to melt it in its own acid. It's slow, hard work, and the acid burns when you touch it. Ram's illness burned away my strength—and also my hair," said Madai, stroking his velvety scalp self-consciously.

"Strange," murmured Sonia. "Why do you say *we* went inside the body?"

"A shining Garuda carried me on its back."

"I see . . ."

Lasmi came bustling into the sleeping house in a flowered sarong, smiling and vigorous. Madai's expression brightened when she appeared. "This is my cousin, Lasmi. She's an herb doctor—and she helps me."

"I'm an herb fan," said Ernie. "Some herbal remedies are baloney, but others really work. Like camomile tea really helps insomnia. I'd like to see your herbs—the best ones."

"We eat mushrooms," said Lasmi shyly.

"I *love mushrooms!*" burbled Ernie. "What kind of mushrooms?"

"These black ones keep you healthy," said Lasmi. "And it's important to eat live cells to stay strong. Right now Madai is only eating live cells."

"Live cells?"

"Food that is still alive when you eat it—raw fruits and vegetables, oysters and curds, foods like that."

"Interesting," said Paul. "Do any of your herbs cure serious illness—like cancer?"

"Only Madai can do that."

Madai's diminutive sister, Dawan, had entered the sleeping house, curious about the foreigners. She stood listening to them, then interrupted in a soft voice. "He cured Ram, but it nearly killed him. See how Madai has changed. I carried him on my hip when he was little. He was always slight, but now he's so thin and his hair is gone. He loved to laugh and dive, and he was *proud* to bring home lobsters. He liked to read and tell stories from the *National Geographic*. Now he lies on his mat, scowling in the heat and brushing away the flies. He used to eat plenty, now he eats so little and he won't go outside —and no wonder! These poor people follow him, grabbing and begging. They camp all night, holding vigils and chanting—even when it rains. Seeing them waiting out there makes me ill myself! And do they really appreciate him? They think that a basket of mealy rice or overripe fruit pays for Madai's trouble. They *never* let him rest, or go diving and grow strong and brown again. We should drive them away! I can hardly tell who is ill and who is the healer. They'll destroy him with their troubles one of these days! Madai respects the knowledge of foreigners—maybe you can talk to him. Maybe you can *help* him."

"How can you drive them away?" sighed Lasmi. "Many are dying and Madai is their last hope. Ketut would have died if Madai had been too busy diving for lobsters."

"Family therapy," Sonia murmured to her husband, Ernie.

"You said a Garuda carried you on its back?" Paul asked Madai.

"Yes, but it's hard to explain. Let's go to my village temple. It's old —maybe you'll like it. It's too hot and noisy inside the house. At the temple I can show you some strange things."

Madai rose up from his sleeping mat, and Lasmi and Dawan glanced at each other with approving little smiles. The foreigners seemed to cheer Madai, and lift him from the stupor that had fallen over him after he healed Ram.

The sick ones squatted in the muddy clearing outside the compound. The monsoon season was approaching and it had been raining hard that week, but they ignored the discomfort. Some had come a long way and waited a long time, and they still waited—they had no other hope. Maybe the wonder-healer would recover his eerie strength if they chanted prayers to the gods. When they saw Madai leave his compound, they tagged after him—was he going to the forest to heal?

"My baby is wasting away with fever," cried a handsome woman.

"My son has malaria, help him," called a gaunt old man.

"This fungus is growing all over my body, please help me, Madai," wept a young girl.

"*Can* you help any of them?" asked Paul.

"I used to—some of them. That's why they still follow me, but now I'm too weak."

As the group walked, a flock of green parrots screamed with surprise to see Madai on his feet again, on the pathway between marshy rice paddies.

"Here is the temple—it's very old. Nobody knows how old, but it was one of the first built on the island when our clan sailed from Bali."

Sonia's face shone with delight. "Look at those immense gateway figures of local Hindu gods, carved with such intricate detail, all overgrown with purple bougainvillea."

Madai flashed a rare smile that lightened his hollow eyes. He always liked it when tourists appreciated the magical old temple.

They entered the mossy, crumbling gateways and explored the ornate pavilions and lavish gardens, with their moist, earthy scents and brilliant equatorial colors. They examined the two delicate, triple-tiered, dark-thatched pagodas that flank the main temple.

"Come inside and I'll show you some things," said Madai.

They entered the dim, massive seven-tiered central pagoda. The humid air buzzed with plump flies attracted to the elaborate fruit and perfumed-flower offerings.

"The big altar in the center is for Brama the Creator," explained Madai. "On one side is the altar for Visnu the Preserver, and the other side holds the altar of Siva the Destroyer. This is our trinity."

"Such strange images," said Sonia. "They've lost the human features of Indian icons and become grotesque gargoyles. Even the Sanskrit names have degraded over time."

"They look damn fierce," said Ernie, twisting his face into a crazed imitation.

"Visnu the Preserver rides on the back of his servant, the Garuda eagle," continued Madai. "A beautiful Garuda carried me on its back for healings—inside the bodies, where it's dark and quiet, like a red cave. There we battled the germbugs, which look like swarming insects, and we were aided only by the mindless, floppy ivory blood cells. Sometimes we found tumors, which grow swiftly as vines. I had to cut them very carefully so I wouldn't harm the flashing nerve strands of sensation. It was very dangerous work."

"I'll bet. Did your Garuda look like that carved wooden image?" asked Paul.

"No," said Madai. "It's made of moonstone and filled with shining colors and light. I carry the image with me—its name is Moonbird. I'll show you . . ." Madai took the glimmering moonstone carving from the silver amulet around his neck.

"Moonbird, that's lovely," smiled Sonia. "How did the Garuda carry you?"

"The Moonbird first came to me when I was a boy. It could carry me on its back anywhere; to the volcano or the moon, under the sea for reef fishing, or even to the Naga realms—and into the bodies for healing."

"He's a classic shamanistic medium, complete with his spirit guide," murmured Paul, studying Madai intently.

A sweet bubbling of gamelan music filled the pagoda.

"Those are the temple dancers and musicians rehearsing for the full moon festival," said Madai. "You can watch them, they like dancing for tourists. Later I'll show you more things."

The foreigners left the thatched temple and entered the garden to watch the performers, who wore gilded brocade sarongs and flower garlands.

The strangers talked quietly among themselves. "His imagination is primitive but so vivid," said Sonia. "He can't accept his psychic powers, so he explains them with simple images. Most shamans first discover their powers as frail children, so his visions are like a charming child's fairy tale."

Paul said, "His descriptions of anatomy are like someone who has never seen an X-ray or a dissection, but saw some pictures in popular magazines. He sees the inside of the body as a red cave, infested with swarming insects or aggressive vines—fascinating. Consider that all these elements are present on this island: large birds, noxious insects, swiftly growing vines. It's easy to trace these naive figments of his imagination. The real question is—*does* he have healing power?" Paul scratched his freckled, sunburned forearm thoughtfully.

Madai trailed behind them, his sensitive hearing picking up every word. So the foreigners didn't believe him; that was disappointing. They thought the Moonbird was a *figment* of his imagination, yet he *liked* these strangers. Their knowledge excited him and he wanted to win their respect. But *how?* For he was still too weak to prove that his healing powers were real.

15

A lively crowd had collected in the temple courtyard to prepare for the forthcoming festival, and to get a head start on the festivities, as the guard-drum throbbed to frighten lurking leyaks.

In a corner of the mossy-walled courtyard, under the imposing guard-drum tower, gathered an excited circle of men. They wore motley combinations of T-shirts and shorts or sarongs, and smoked clove-scented kratek cigarettes.

Ernie wandered over to see what was happening, and found that two of the men held fighting cocks, one white and one russet, their legs adorned with long, wicked-looking spikes of polished steel. The men examined the cocks to see if they were evenly matched, and to be sure the blades were properly bound. The onlookers shouted their bets with shining black eyes, and boldly tossed coins and rumpled bills into the circle.

The crowd fell silent as the cocks were placed in the center of the ring and released. The birds leaped and twisted in a flurry of aerial combat, slashing at each other with lightning speed. The russet cock struck at the white's head with his lethal spurs—and it collapsed in a twitching heap of bloody white feathers. The battle was over within moments, and the winners took their money with elated grins while the losers retreated in sullen silence.

"They permit cockfighting in the temple?" Ernie asked Madai, who was still grumbling about *figments* under his breath.

"Oh yes, the temple is a meeting place for all the people of the desa. These cocks have been groomed by their owners for years to fight before the festival. Their blood is a sacrifice to the leyak spirits, so they won't interfere with the ceremonies. And gaming is popular on the island. Some men lose their land from too much gambling."

On a platform under a grove of fragrant pink-flowered frangipani trees, the musicians and dancers gathered in a kaleidoscope of harmonious color and sound while large-eyed children clustered below, aping their movements.

Sonia said, "See how the children learn the dance movements

when they're small—that's why they move with such effortless grace. When westerners try to learn these dances it looks so clumsy and forced."

The musicians wore brown and white batik sarongs and headbands, and played their instruments with rhythmic vitality. Many were older men, with white hair, tissue-paper skin, and hollow faces. There were two large drums, the male and female, covered with water buffalo hide. They were balanced in the laps of the cross-legged players, who controlled the tempo of the floating music with tireless hands and wooden sticks. The contrapuntal melody was woven by the xylophone-like gamelans made of intricately carved jackwood, metal, and bamboo. The players focused intently on their bronze keyboards, using both hands to create and mute the complicated patterns of notes. Rows of polished metal gongs, set on ornately carved wooden bases, were played by four musicians as a bubbling ornamentation. Cymbals crashed with excitement. Haunting flutes, and the *rebab*, a sweet-voiced two stringed violin, completed the magical orchestra.

The dancers flowed onto the platform, their bodies swathed in lustrous brocade, their tall gilded headdresses woven with sweet frangipani. Their faces were painted into stylized masks of white, black, and red. They moved with measured steps and bent knees, their heads tilted and their eyes and faces blank—ready to be entered and animated by the spirits of the characters they portrayed. Their arms were lifted gracefully, and their fingers trembled and gestured with symbolic meaning as they enacted the ancient Indian tale of the *Ramayana*.

Rama and Laksmana, played by two handsome young women, danced the tale of their exile in the forest . . . Rama, wearing a golden crown, and Laksmana in a black headdress, moved with stately refinement. Rama had been heir to the kingdom of Ayodhya, but was deprived of his crown by his wicked stepmother, and banished to the forest of Dendaka in the high Himalayas. His loyal wife, Sita, and his brave brother, Laksmana, insisted on accompanying the dethroned prince. Deep in the woods they found asylum with saintly hermits, who gave Rama a magic bow to subdue the forest ogres. They built a hut in a clearing and lived there peacefully for thirteen years.

This was the story told by the stylized gestures of the beautifully costumed dancers, and the white-robed *pemangu* priest, chanting in the ancient Javanese poetic language of *Kawi*.

Dusk shadowed the island, and the crowd of onlookers grew as the workday ended. Raucous crows wheeled and called overhead, seeking roosts for the night. Kerosene lamps were lit in the courtyard, and little food stands appeared outside the massive, crumbling temple gates, selling fragrant kebabs and peppery fried rice. Chanting crickets, frogs, and geckos harmonized with the floating music. Families and skinny dogs curled up at the base of the pavilion to watch the dress rehearsal. Young men and women eyed each other with flirtatious smiles, and children frolicked.

Ernie sniffed the air appreciatively, then scurried out to check the food stands. He staggered back with mounds of spicy fried rice, shrimp, and onions on banana leaves; bottles of Australian beer, grilled pork on bamboo skewers, and other exotic goodies. He settled down with Sonia, Paul, and Madai to watch the dancers while he ate—and ate.

Madai felt excited but weary. This was the longest he'd been away from his compound since he'd healed Ram. Lasmi joined them, and he rested his smooth bald head against her soft arm. The dancers and musicians wove their tale, heedless of the life that pulsed beneath them.

The demonic ten-headed giant, Rawana, discovered Rama's peaceful forest aerie, and was captivated by Sita's grace and beauty. Urged on by his evil sister, who had been spurned by the brothers, he plotted to kidnap Sita. Rawana sent his evil minister, disguised as a golden deer, to lure the brothers away from Sita. The lithe boy dancer costumed as the golden deer pranced gaily across the platform and shook his horns enticingly. Sita urged Rama to fetch the enchanting creature for her. Leaving Laksmana to guard his wife, Rama followed the deer. It lured him deep into the forest, eluding his grasp. Finally Rama grew suspicious, and shot the deer with his magic bow. The deer fell to the ground and resumed the grotesque form of the evil minister, but before it died it bellowed in Rama's voice. Laksmana heard his brother's cry and boldly set out to the rescue, marching across the platform with glaring eyes.

When both brothers were gone, a blast of wind shook the hut, and Rawana appeared with the red eyes in his ten monstrously tusked heads blazing with desire. He swept struggling Sita into the air, and carried her to his fortress in Lanka. A dancer who was exquisitely costumed as a bright green Garuda tried to rescue Sita, but was mortally wounded by the demon. Before it collapsed in a flutter of green feathers, the Garuda told sorrowing Rama where Sita had gone. The cymbals clashed as Rama and Laksmana set out in search of her, their long fingers trembling with rage.

On their way they met the magnificent white-furred monkey warrior Hanuman, whose King had been deprived of his rightful throne. Rama used his magic bow to help the monkey King destroy his enemies and regain the crown. In a proud dance of gratitude, the monkey King ordered Hanuman to lead the monkey troop in search of Sita.

The nearly full moon floated over the mossy temple wall, and a moist, warm breeze ruffled the scented frangipani. The toddlers and dogs had dozed off, and reckless night insects buzzed around the flickering kerosene lanterns. The stone carvings became shadowy apparitions as the musicians sat lean and intent over their instruments, twining sound. Women arranged towers of fruit and flowers, and elaborate dough figures, as festival offerings. Ernie wandered back outside the gate, and bought sweet rice and coconut cakes, sliced fresh fruit bathed in sugar, ginger and chilis, and rich Java coffee. Sonia and Paul sat fascinated by the drama. Madai dreamily rested against Lasmi and wondered if his powers had ever been real, and the dancers were immersed in their own reality.

Hanuman's monkey armies searched the world for Sita. When they reached Lanka, white-furred Hanuman leaped across the strait to the walled garden of Rawana's immense fortress. There he found mournful Sita, and they danced together with tilted heads and expressive gestures as he gave her Rama's ring in promise that she would be rescued. Mighty Hanuman grew a hundredfold, bellowed a warning to the demons, and set Rawana's capital afire with his breath. The monkey army shouted their rhythmic chant . . . *chak* . . . *chak* . . . *chak* . . . as they built a bridge of boulders to invade Lanka.

The village men who had watched the cockfight had changed their motley clothes for the black-and-white checkered loincloths of the proud monkey army. They wore nothing else except a white spot of paint on their foreheads, and a white flower over their right ears. The white-robed *pemangu* priest had chanted prayers while fanning incense smoke from a brazier over them, to induce the trance state that allowed the spirits of the ancient monkey warriors to enter and possess their bodies. Their eyes glazed over and the troop leaped upon the platform, carrying blazing torches and shouting the pounding *chak . . . chak . . . chak* with an eerie rhythm. The monkey army circled struggling Hanuman and Rawana in a living coil, their waving torches casting strange shadows. They raised their arms and swayed back and forth in dramatic unison, furiously battling a vast army of invisible demons, while the pulsing *chak . . . chak . . . chak* reached an ecstatic crescendo.

Rama stomped onto the platform with fiery eyes, aimed his magic bow, and killed the monster, Rawana. The great battle ended and the chanting of the monkey army quieted. The priest sprinkled the village men with holy water to waken them from their trance.

Rama, Sita, and Laksmana triumphantly returned to their kingdom in Rawana's flying chariot. In a regal dance, Rama regained his throne, and became the wisest King of Ayodhya.

"The play is ended, but the story goes on forever . . ." sang the priest, holding up a large leaf of filigreed leather and silver to signal the end of the drama.

The music trailed into silence, and the dress rehearsal of the two-thousand-year-old tale ended. The dancers removed their swaying headdresses, wiped off their stylized makeup, and became smiling villagers again. Vendors packed up their pots and doused their charcoal braziers, and the musicians prepared their instruments to take home. Mothers woke up their children and gathered babies in their arms. The moon was high and the trade winds were brisk as the crowd meandered out of the shadowy temple courtyard.

"I hope that government guesthouse has hot showers and comfortable beds; I'm beat," said Ernie with a yawn. "And I have raging indigestion—maybe I ate too much fried rice."

"Before my brother guides you to the guesthouse, let me take you inside the temple to show you one more thing," said Madai.

16

Madai led the three inquisitive foreigners back inside the main temple pagoda, holding a fluttering kerosene lamp that illuminated the blackness around them with grotesque shadows.

"What do you think causes disease?" asked Madai.

"Germs, injury, degeneration—things like that," replied Ernie.

"We also believe in those things," said Madai. "We have filth-borne infections carried by the germbugs. They're easy to heal. There are ailments caused by natural decay, which nobody can heal. We have two causes which you do not recognize. One is afflictions caused by actions in past lives, such as deformed infants, that nobody can cure. There is one more cause of misfortune which is very strange."

"What's that?" asked Paul.

"Maladies caused by demons and evil spirits. On this island we have one very wicked spirit who causes much suffering. You see the altar of Siva the Destroyer? One of his servants is Rangda the witch. She is covered with this white cloth to contain her evil, but I will lift it up and show her face to you. See how ugly she is, with her bulging eyes and curved fangs, her splintery claws and matted hair. She denies that she causes disasters—but she's always there when trouble occurs."

As Madai spoke, some of his old boyish animation returned. Despite his weariness, he was eager to discuss his ideas with these knowledgeable and interesting strangers.

"She *talks* to you? Oh, that's fascinating," said Sonia. "The carved wooden mask is a beautiful piece of traditional island art. I love these antiques—I wonder how old it is. Let me take a closer look."

"No!" cried Madai, his eyes wide with fear.

It was already too late. As Sonia Spiegle, Ph.D., of California U.S.A., reached out to touch Rangda's coppery hair, Madai saw the white tusked face flicker with a blue glow. The clawed hands trembled, and the bulging eyes stared with cold and malevolent surprise.

"I *see*," hissed Rangda.

"*Beh!* Don't say that!" shouted Madai. He tried to push Sonia aside, but she stumbled forward in the darkness. Ernie reached out to grab her, and they both toppled against the image of Rangda—which smashed onto the cobbled temple floor. It landed with a thud and cracked into several large pieces.

"Be careful!" said Paul. "Are you all right, Sonia?"

"Just a little shaken. I'm afraid I've smashed a local icon—and upset our healer."

"Don't worry," said Ernie. "We have plenty of money. We'll pay to have it repaired."

The research group finally returned to the rustic government guesthouse near the dock. It was a simple, stilted white wooden bungalow with a red tin roof, furnished with narrow metal cots, a rough table and chairs, and local ebony carvings. There was a weathered outhouse perched over the creek in back, and bathing was done with buckets of tepid river water fetched by the guesthouse attendants, who could also prepare tasty meals of fish, rice, and fruit.

Dreams of hot showers evaporated as the trio washed from the buckets. In the wavering light of Coleman lamps, they sat flossing their teeth as a forlorn gesture to civilization, and comparing their notes for the day.

"He's a strange chap but I like him," said Paul, sipping tea from a dented metal cup.

"He seems honest and sincere, and I think he enjoys talking to us," said Ernie. "The other healers we've met were all so glib and boastful, and eager to prove their powers. He's almost casual about the whole thing, as if it's perfectly natural to ride a shining bird inside other people's bodies." Ernie burped softly.

"Apparently his last healing emotionally drained him, and he's depressed by those pitiful people following him around. He's afraid he lost his boyhood vision of the bird spirit who gave him his powers, so he just mopes around his house," said Sonia, combing her silvered hair.

"I wonder if we could snap him out of it," mused Paul. "I'd love to see a demonstration, and I'm sure it would help the poor devil's morale. Then there's always the minute chance that he might help Jana in some way. We could offer him a good bit of money—that might boost him out of his depression and get him functioning again." He lit a mosquito-repellent coil that produced a lazy spiral of scented smoke.

"I hope the islanders won't turn against us because I broke that idol in the temple. Madai seemed absolutely terrified," said Sonia, looking troubled.

"I think he wanted to protect you from the demoness," smiled Paul. "He's a likable chap. Let's stay a while and persuade him to show us a healing."

"Let's not stay *too* long," grumbled Sonia irritably, her face looking strangely flushed and sweaty. "These accommodations are beastly. I'd love to get back to that gorgeous hotel on Bali. This place is crawling with bugs, and I'm convinced that our washing water came from the same filthy creek that runs under the outhouse. Be careful at those grimy food stands, Ernie."

"Come on, Sonia, you've always been an intrepid explorer, you can rough it for a few days," said Ernie, looking at his wife in surprise. "We'll use chlorine tablets in the water, and feast on ripe fruit plucked by tawny maidens. This is a wonderful adventure! We've found a despairing healer who flies on a shiny bird to battle demons and disease—it's like a fairy tale."

"I suppose I can manage," grumped Sonia, wiping her face. She felt a sudden wave of dizziness, and her whole body was drenched with clammy sweat. She clutched the edge of the wooden table, waiting for the swoon to pass. "I *see* . . ." she murmured.

"Is something wrong, Sonia?" asked Paul.

"Just some nausea . . . This island is too *weird* for me." Then Sonia Spiegle, Ph.D., of California, U.S.A., choked and vomited violently on the table and floor—and collapsed.

By dawn, Sonia lay delirious on the metal cot, in the rustic government guesthouse near the dock. She had a very high fever, and coughed and retched. Though she badly needed bottled drinks from the Chinese store to prevent dehydration, she was unable to keep them down.

Ernest Spiegle, M.D., of California, U.S.A., developed a milder case of what seemed to be dysentery. He remained conscious and could sip tinned juice, but complained of feeling feverish, nauseous, and irritable. His infamous appetite disappeared, and he made frequent trips to the outhouse.

Paul Robbes, Ph.D., professor of anthropology from Rotorua, New Zealand, showed no signs of infection. He hovered anxiously around the ailing pair, rummaging for pills in the medicine kit, buying soft drinks and juice from the Chinese store, and consulting with the missionaries and the small enclave of government officials.

"Father Hans says that severe dysentery is rare on this island," said Paul to Ernie, who lay on his cot looking weak and sallow. "The nuns say the islanders have a simple but effective means of keeping their water supplies pure. Only certain streams are used for sewage. The river and ponds are used for washing, while only pure springs are saved for cooking and drinking. Maybe you picked it up in India, which is much dirtier."

"Let's get out of here!" said Ernie. "Sonia needs a hospital with antibiotics and intravenous fluids—or she might not make it." He began to cough.

"I've made inquiries," said Paul, a worried expression on his paternal, bearded face. "The mail boat only sails once a week."

"A *week!*" cried Ernie. "I can last that long, but Sonia is seriously ill. Go talk to the bloody officials. Tell them to radio for a helicopter to pick us up from Bali. We'll pay whatever the bandits want."

"I already tried that," said Paul. "They say it's impossible. If we can't wait for the mail boat, we must rent a fishing boat. I went down to the dock to look, and they're all flimsy little outboard dugouts. The channel is rough now, with the monsoon approaching. I'm concerned that we wouldn't make it beyond the reefs. It seems risky to me—and I'm a seasoned sailor."

"That's *crazy!* Sonia could die if we don't get out of here. Bribe the officials to get us a helicopter."

In her cot, Sonia lay with sweat running down her face, her eyes tightly closed, muttering to herself. ". . . I see matted copper hair," she mumbled. "I see . . ."

Madai sat tensely in the stifling thatched sleeping house, swatting marauding insects and waiting for them to reappear. The foreigners had promised to return early in the morning to talk to him. Now it was nearly afternoon and they still hadn't arrived.

He was disappointed. Maybe they didn't like him—didn't believe that he once had healing powers. He was eager to talk with them; their conversations yesterday had stimulated his mind. It was the first return of vitality and interest since he'd healed Ram.

They were educated and modern, and had traveled everywhere. They could tell him about the healers of India and the Philippines, and the scientific marvels of America. They could discuss causes and cures—and they wanted to learn from *him*. Madai was keenly interested in learning from them. He paced around the house and the walled compound, waiting impatiently for them to appear.

Finally he sent Ketut to the guesthouse to make inquiries. His sunken eyes looked frightened when he heard that two of the foreigners were ill. He marched resolutely along the palm-lined riverside pathway to the dock as a small band of imploring sick ones tagged after him. He found the foreigners in the guesthouse, looking grim.

"What happened?" asked Madai.

"Dysentery," said Paul. "Ernie will pull through, but Sonia is in very bad shape, severely dehydrated. We don't know how long she can last without hospitalization, and there's no way to get off this damn island. You're supposed to be a healer—*do* something."

"I told you I lost my power. Maybe Lasmi can brew some herbs . . ."

"Well get your bloody power back! We'll pay you well—if that's what interests you."

Madai's pride was hurt. "No, money isn't what interests me," he said stiffly.

"Sorry, we'll pay you anyway. We're desperate and we'll try anything. You *must* help us."

Madai went to Sonia's bed, stroked her forehead with his sinewy hand, and massaged the pulses in her wrists. She lay curled in a fetal posture, her black and silver hair in disarray, breathing hoarsely and muttering, ". . . I see matted copper hair."

"She keeps saying that," said Ernie.

"*Rangda!*" cried Madai. "I must go now . . ."

The foreigners stared in surprise as the frail healer in the faded cotton sarong hurried out the guesthouse door.

"I see . . ." whimpered Sonia.

17

Madai raced to the village temple. The image of Rangda lay on the altar, broken into large shards. The priests and master carvers would carefully restore the ancient wooden effigy, but work hadn't begun yet. Heaps of flowers and fruit and smoky incense offerings were piled at the base of the altar to placate the witch's wrath.

The broken mask was severed from the body. The largest shard included an eye, a cheek, and the mouth, and most of the skull with its long, tangled hair. The rest of Rangda's face was cracked into irregular pieces.

Madai addressed the fragments on the altar. "Are you still alive, witch? Why did you make the foreigners ill?"

There was no answer. The shards lay desolately while rotund green flies buzzed randomly around the wilted offerings.

"Antagonist, I know you're still there. Nobody can destroy you. Answer me."

The largest shard—with the tufts of hair, one bulging eye, and the mouth—flickered with a blue glow. The single eye stared at him with cold rancor and pain.

". . . Shattered me . . . Hurts so . . ." slurred a breathy hiss.

"You threatened the foreign woman when she tried to touch you," said Madai.

"No threats . . . Only saw . . ."

"Then why did the two foreigners who touched you get sick, while the other remains well? You *lie*, Rangda."

"No lies . . . Smashed me . . . Can't fix . . . hurts so . . ." the icy eye stared at him with fearful malice.

"So even Rangda can suffer," said Madai. He hurried out of the carved temple gateway.

Madai stood outside the sandstone walls, trying to decide. Should he return home and rest? Or should he go to the clearing in the forest, among the groves of banyans and bamboos, to stare at the glowing moonstone image and summon the Moonbird to heal the foreigners?

"I no longer have any power, I'm too weak," he murmured, starting back to his stuffy, noisy house.

Yet maybe one more time I can ride the Moonbird, he thought. *Dysentery is easy to cure. Then they'll believe I have power and talk to me more. Otherwise they'll say I'm fake and the Moonbird is figment, and go quickly away. I want to talk to them and learn. Maybe I can ride the Moonbird— one more time.*

Madai headed into the forest. His younger brother and a handful of sick ones patiently followed behind. "Go to the guesthouse," he told Ketut. "Tell them I'll *try* to cure the woman, but I cannot promise anything. *Hurry.* Don't stop to play games with your friends."

Madai's brother scampered off with a wide grin, envisioning a big tip for himself.

The sick ones chattered like excited monkeys when they heard Madai's words. They clutched at him, begging him to heal them too. The pretty woman with the sick baby fell in the mud and tried to kiss his bare feet. He shook them off.

"I'll *try,*" he snapped. "I can't help anybody if you hang around pestering me."

They stood back and watched with tearful, pleading faces as the slight healer walked alone into the forest. He sat cross-legged in the familiar clearing. It had been months since he'd visited this place. He fished the small moonstone carving from the silver amulet around his neck, and held it up to a slanting beam of sunlight so that the stone glowed with inner fire.

He stared and stared—but nothing happened.

Paul returned with Ketut to observe the healing.

"I'm sorry," said Madai, with a look of shame on his hollow face. "The Moonbird will not come to me. I have no more power."

Paul watched Madai for a while, then grew impatient and left. Madai stared and waited with a growing sense of hopelessness as sullen mosquitoes circled him with mocking whines.

It was almost dusk and Madai was alone. He had fallen into a semidoze, but was startled awake by a strange and exhilarating surge of power racing up his spine—and the rustle of soft wings. The shimmering Moonbird appeared before him.

"Where were you?" asked Madai, leaping up to hug the Garuda's shining neck.

"Very far from here."

"On the moon?"

"Much farther than that . . ."

"Well, I'm awfully glad to see you again. Can you still carry me to do healings? The American woman is very ill."

The Moonbird appraised Madai with gleaming eyes. "You look thin and weak, but we can try."

The bullfrogs and crickets had begun their evening plainchant. Madai's legs felt stiff from his long vigil, and the spiteful mosquitoes had attacked his bare head. He climbed slowly onto the Moonbird's back, enjoying the cool touch of the smooth feathers, for he had missed the Moonbird.

The Garuda tensed its muscles and rose up over the banyans and bamboos. They sailed above the tin-roofed guesthouse—and time and space coiled as they entered the body of Dr. Sonia, who lay curled and mumbling on her cot.

"Something's *moving* inside me!" cried Sonia sharply.

"She's still delirious," sighed Paul, who sat at the rough table watching her. It was growing dark and he lit a Coleman lamp.

"I'm filled with light," wept Sonia, her eyes tightly closed.

Ketut ran panting into the room. "I went to fetch Madai for his supper, but I couldn't wake him. He's entered the healing trance, rocking and mumbling in the forest. The lady will be better soon."

"You mean he's healing her right now?" asked Paul, rushing over to the cot.

Ernie put down a bowl of imported cream of asparagus soup, from a dusty tin Paul had found at the Chinese store, and sat up eagerly in his bed.

"Full of *light*," moaned Sonia.

Then she opened her eyes for the first time since she'd collapsed the previous night. She saw the others clustered around her and smiled at them weakly. "I'm terribly thirsty," she said.

Paul reached over and touched her forehead. "Her fever has finally broken," he said.

"That was simple," smiled Madai to the Moonbird as they rose up from the guesthouse. "Those bacteria are like big, squishy jellyfish. I can pop them like bubbles with my bare feet."

Madai wrapped his thin brown arms around the long, gleaming neck of the Moonbird. "I'm so glad to be with you again. It feels so good to fly on your back and battle the germbugs. Maybe soon we could go to the beach," he said wistfully. "I haven't gone diving for a long time. I'm bored sitting at home and it gives me a headache. Tomorrow let's dive for lobsters—but first we should heal the sick ones who are waiting outside my house."

"You want to heal them all—*now?*" asked the Moonbird in a surprised whisper. "Are you strong enough? Perhaps you should rest at the beach."

"Gods mustn't be lazy," laughed Madai. "We'll go to the beach tomorrow. I feel much stronger now. Let's start with that poor crying baby, I think there's fluid in her ears, causing her fever and giving her pain. There's an old woman with bad kidneys, and a boy with worms, and an infected lung. The others are sadly hopeless. I feel so lively again. I've been resting too long—we'll help as many as we can."

"Dynamite!" said Paul. "That baby's ear and the old woman's kidneys have cleared up like magic."

After Madai had sat in the forest for two days, rocking and nodding in a healing trance, everyone grew worried. His family hovered anxiously around the muddy clearing, shooed vindictive mosquitoes, moistened his lips with coco-water, and tried to waken him without success. The foreigners worried too. They wanted to notify their sponsor, Jana Davids, that they'd met a promising healer. What was the problem? Why wouldn't he wake up?

They went to the forest and watched him nervously. They thrust smelling salts under his nose and waved their flashlights into his eyes. They called to him and pinched his cool, immobile limbs without any response.

"The stress of the healings has caused a classic catatonic depression," said Sonia, who had regained enough strength to hike into the forest and observe Madai, rocking and mumbling in the clearing.

"Just my luck," sighed Paul. "I finally found my miracle worker—and he's batty as a nut tree."

"He'll die of thirst and exposure if he stays there much longer," said Ernie, who had recovered from his own malaise, and was crunching rice crackers.

Madai's family sadly agreed. Soon word flowed throughout the desas. Madai had tried to regain his powers—and now he was dying in the forest.

Madai completed the healings, then he rested, hovering in a translucent blue void upon the shimmering Moonbird. His frail arms wound around the Garuda's long neck, and his cheek was buried in the smooth, cool feathers. He felt no discomfort or need. He felt only a deep and soothing peace that cleansed and refreshed his mind.

There was only the calming, cobalt blue. Madai was very far away . . .

Gradually he realized that his body was growing lighter and weaker, and that he might perish if he remained floating in the peaceful blue. He lifted his head, which felt heavy. When he moved his arm, it trembled. "Moonbird, I'm hungry and thirsty," he said through papery lips. "I need water and fruit."

The Moonbird obligingly spread its wings and descended from the crystalline blue, which grew deeper and warmer as a wind whined in his ears. Soon it was the intense blue of a sunny tropical sky, and when Madai looked down he could see the deep green of the island hills. He had returned from the void, but he was starving.

They landed in a mountainside grove of wild banana trees, fed by a bubbling spring. He was ravenous. He drank and drank, and ate the sweet, creamy little bananas until he could hold no more. He felt better immediately and the trembling ceased.

"Two more people have reported that all their symptoms are gone," said Ernie, munching a mango. "Madai is swaying and mumbling less, and his skin has a more normal tone. Our healer may have emotional problems—but I think he's coming around."

On the late afternoon of the third day, Madai opened his eyes and found his family, the foreigners, and villagers hovering around him. His neck was heaped with fragrant flower garlands from grateful families of those he'd healed. Piles of gifts and offerings were strewn at his feet.

"Good morning," Madai said to the gathered crowd. His mother, Dawan, and Lasmi wept and hugged him.

"You're awake!" cried Sonia. "How do you feel? My dysentery is gone—but you must be terribly thirsty and hungry."

"I'm all right," shrugged Madai. "Just a little tired from so many healings. But the Moonbird gave me a big lunch of sweet bananas and cool spring water." The strangers laughed with surprise, and the villagers carried Madai on their shoulders to his house.

18

"It hurts us so . . ." hissed the wrathful shards of Rangda.

"His delusional system is naive, but he may have real psychic powers—and I like him," said Sonia as they climbed the wicker stairway to Madai's sleeping house.

"Of course the healings *could* have been coincidental," said Ernie, peeling an orange.

"Sudden recovery from virulent dysentery isn't ordinary," said Sonia. "And I had that strange, distinct sensation of light moving inside me."

"That was probably delirium," said Ernie.

"Maybe it was my flashlight," said Madai from his sleeping mat.

"Your flashlight?" asked Paul. "Do you use your torch in the healings?"

"Oh yes, it's very dark inside the bodies. I need the light to see, and it stops the germbugs from moving so much."

They chuckled and Madai looked at them, puzzled. He'd expected gratitude, not laughter.

"I'm sorry, Madai," smiled Sonia. "It's just such an odd image: a healer armed with a flashlight, flying on a shining bird inside me. We have such mystical associations with light. It sounds strange when you speak of a simple flashlight."

Madai flicked on his flashlight with a shy grin, and shone it around the room, which was lined with low shelves and woven straw mats. They all laughed.

"So what was it like inside my stomach?" asked Sonia.

"It looked nice and healthy," said Madai. "Maybe a little bit pale—Lasmi can brew some herbs to strengthen your blood."

"True, I'm a bit anemic. How did you cure me?"

"I fixed those dysentery jellyfish with my flashlight and popped them like bubbles, one by one."

"You mean you popped *each* bacterium? That must take a long time—and how did you fit inside?" asked Sonia.

"Time and space bend—like rubber."

"Fascinating," said Paul. "He uses such simplistic visual images, but something *real* is happening here."

They all stared at him now as if he weren't quite solid.

"You say you've cured cancer?" asked Ernie.

"Yes, but that's not so easy. Cancer is very powerful; Ram was so sick he could hardly walk. He almost died—and his tumor made me bald. Now he's quite well—but my hair never grew back." He touched his smooth scalp wistfully.

"You see, Madai, we have a special reason for asking so many questions," said Paul. "We've traveled all over Asia looking for healers. Many people *say* they can cure illness, but mostly they're fakes—either fools or cheats. It's so rare to find someone like you whose cures seem to *work*. Your explanations are, well, *odd*. But this didn't seem like coincidence or placebo effect. Sonia was unconscious and severely ill. We were worried she'd die here. Then you went into the woods to talk to your birds, and now she's recovering nicely—and so are four others who were waiting outside your house with serious ailments."

"I only talk to *one* bird," said Madai.

"Right, I forgot," said Paul. "We have a friend who is paying for our search. She's very rich and powerful—and very ill with lung cancer. She asked us to find someone to cure her. I think you and Jana Davids will like each other a lot, and if you were successful she'd do anything to reward you. We want to send her a message to come here, to the island. Her jet can fly to Bali, and she can charter a yacht from there. Would you be willing to see her—and to try to heal her?"

Madai nodded hesitantly.

"Let's telegraph word to Jana," said Paul.

"Hurts us so . . ." whimpered Rangda.

The shards of the witch lay sullenly on the altar in the midday heat, surrounded by buzzing flies, and grew angrier and angrier. Then Rangda's wrath slowly took form . . .

The immense water buffalo demon, Mahisha, appeared on the slopes of Mount Alāka, and bellowed Rangda's fury. The ferocious buffalo stamped his mighty hooves and a sharp earthquake shivered the island, uprooting trees, collapsing village compounds, and sending massive waves pounding onto the rickety dock.

"What's happening?" cried Sonia as Madai's sleeping house careened crazily, and people shouted and screamed below.

"*Beh!* Earthquake," said Madai. "Come outside."

They made their way down the jouncing wicker ladder. The ground swayed under their feet, then trembled wearily and grew still.

The people of the desa surveyed the damage. Venerable fruit trees and mud walls had been destroyed, and pigs and ruffled chickens scampered nervously along the muddy village pathways. Dwellings sagged on toppled stilts. There was a gaping crack in the carved sandstone gateway of the temple. The people stood in worried knots, discussing how to repair the damage.

Mahisha stamped his hooves again, and another shock slammed through the island. When it subsided, more houses and orchards had been destroyed. Part of the wooden dock was swept away by the high surf. The glass windows of the Chinese store and mission school were shattered. There was extensive damage to the irrigation system that fed the vital rice paddies. One of the temple gates had collapsed into a pile of sandstone rubble.

Mahisha shook his enormous head, and the corona of fierce gnats that live off the demon's blood rose up in a great black whirling cloud, and descended upon the villagers with insatiable greed.

"Bloody God!" cried Paul as the foreigners frantically sprayed each other with insect repellent.

Mahisha snorted a vast puff of steam through his huge, crusted nostrils. The steam became a murky storm cloud. Lightning cracked from the mountainsides to the forests. A maniacal wind splintered the trees, and a deluge inundated the island, uprooting the rice crop. The Waringan River overflowed its banks, and swept away the fishing shacks along its shores as Mahisha thundered his demonic rage.

When the typhoon subsided, the islanders dashed around, swatting stray gnats and trying to salvage what they could. The foreigners huddled fearfully inside a sturdy storage hut in Madai's family compound.

Madai and the village men were unhappily surveying the damaged temple walls, when a troop of large monkeys came racing from the forest along the jagged, broken branches of the tallest trees. Their leader was a big albino male, with white fur and an oddly clipped tail.

"*Chak* . . . *Chak* . . . *Chak* . . . Mahisha will destroy the island if we can't stop him!" the leader of the monkey troop shrieked to Madai.

"*Hanuman!*" called Madai in wonder.

"Perhaps that was my name long ago, when my tail was graceful and strong," said the white-furred monkey leader wistfully. "I've had so many names I can't remember them all. I lost my tail ages ago through boundless curiosity, and now I romp carelessly among the fruit trees of our island. Today my mind was roused by the cruel water buffalo, Mahisha, who was summoned by the vengeful witch to stand upon the volcano's summit and shower disasters upon us. I have come to warn you, man-child. The demon must be destroyed, or he'll annihilate our peaceful island. Yet no drop of his blood must touch the ground, lest the sleeping volcano spirits be roused and obliterate us with deadly fire."

"How can the water buffalo be ravaged without bloodshed?" asked Madai.

"*Chak . . . Chak . . .* You must join us, man-child," said the white monkey. He and his troop flitted away through the shattered treetops.

Madai abruptly left the damaged temple, and laboriously made his way through a tangle of uprooted trees to his banyan and bamboo clearing, which was littered with debris.

He quickly summoned the Moonbird, and they flew to the desolate upper slopes of Mount Alāka. They hovered in the chill winds and saw the massive gray form of Mahisha preparing to rattle the island with his mighty hooves once again.

There was movement among the stunted conifers that ring the lava-crusted summit. The monkey troop appeared among the trees, riding the back of Barong, the lion-headed dragon who guards the island.

"*Chak . . . Chak . . . Chak . . .*" called the monkey troop, dragging a thick tangle of vines from the dense lower forests.

The buffalo demon lifted his hoof with a snort, and prepared to smash it into the blackened ground. At that moment the clip-tailed white monkey whipped a long vine tendril through the air so it curled around Mahisha's upraised leg.

"Grab the loose end and pull it tight!" shrieked the white monkey to Madai and the Moonbird.

The Garuda swooped down, and Madai leaned forward to grasp the end of the vine that twisted around the monster's leg. The

Moonbird gripped it with a powerful claw and they all pulled hard against the vine, which tightened like a rope around Mahisha's leg and unbalanced the water buffalo, crashing him to the ground and sending shock waves through the island.

"Tie him up like a calf at the sacrificial altar! But don't break his hide—if he bleeds one drop we all die!" shrilled the clip-tailed monkey leader.

The monkeys raced from the thin upper forests with their heavy vines, and lashed the legs of the thrashing water buffalo. Mahisha opened his mouth wide and bellowed long and loud, which caused waterspouts to rise up in the sea, and whirlwinds to whip around the island.

"Let's tie his mouth!" said Madai. He grabbed a strong vine, and twined it in loose loops around the demon's gaping jaws. The Moonbird grasped both ends of the vine in its beak and pulled them tight . . . *tighter.* Until Mahisha's mouth was forced shut, and the whirlwinds died down.

The water buffalo thrashed his tail and a huge surf crashed along the shore, destroying the little fishing piers.

Lion-headed Barong, his coat aglitter with flecks of mica, pranced and feinted like a bullfighter at Mahisha's head to distract the demon while the white monkey lassoed the tail and tied it to the beast's hindquarters.

They trussed the struggling creature with the ropelike vines until he looked like a great brute ready for slaughter.

"We can't kill him, for we mustn't shed his blood," said Madai. "What will we do? He's too big and dangerous to tame to the plow— but we can't stay here, holding these vines forever."

"*Chak . . . Chak . . .* Throw him in the sea!" shrieked the monkeys.

"He's so heavy," said Madai. "How can we move him?"

"Let me try," said the Moonbird, carefully gathering the ends of the vines in its beak. With great effort, the shimmering Garuda lifted the bound buffalo demon into the air, trailing his droning halo of insect parasites. Flying low and wobbling over the trees, they descended from the slopes of the volcano, and flew over the wasted green forests. The Moonbird could barely stay aloft. Madai feared they would plunge into the splintered foliage, tearing the monster's hide with sharp branches, and provoking the fiery volcano spirits to rain death upon them.

Finally the sea appeared beneath them, still storm dark and turbulent, and filled with tossing rubbish. The white monkey and his chattering troop leaped from Barong's sinuous back, into the blasted coco-palms that line the beach.

Beyond the coral reef, the great winged turtle, Bedawang, awaited them. "Mahanagini, the cobra-hooded Naga Queen, is annoyed with this beast, for she has felt the tempest even in her deep and calm realm. She asked me to take the reins which bind the water buffalo and lead him to her. She has spells to tame rebellious creatures, and she'll use him to plow the golden fields of kelp," said the turtle, taking the vine ropes from the Moonbird in his mighty parrot's beak.

The monkeys bounced up and down in the trees with raucous *chaks* as Bedawang pulled gasping Mahisha under the waves.

"The monsoon really gets heavy on these islands," said Ernie, gnawing the creamy meat of a downed coconut.

"We've already wired Jana detailed instructions on getting here, and now the lines are down, so we can't stop her," fretted Sonia.

"She'll find quite a mess," nodded Paul.

19

The sleek white yacht moved with inexorable grace toward the hastily repaired dock, its blue-and-white-striped sail billowing in the trade winds. When it anchored, there was no clamor of vendors offering snacks and trinkets, for the people were busy cleaning their storm-shattered island. The three foreigners, and Madai and his family, were the only greeting party.

Madai's family pointed and jabbered with surprise. They had never seen such a handsome boat. With its motors and sail, it had skimmed along the water like a gull. Now it rested gaily at anchor, its tall masts gleaming in the sunlight. The Balinese crew busily tended to their tasks while the lone passenger prepared to disembark with her attendant nurse.

Red-headed Ernie, his wife, Sonia, and the bearded New Zealander, Paul Robbes, waited at the foot of the dock and greeted the passenger with warm and effusive hugs. Madai and his family followed shyly.

Madai's sunken black eyes fixed on the newcomer. This was Jana Davids, the woman they'd asked him to heal. She was long and rangy. Her face was gaunt and her flesh was wasted with disease. Yet the tremendous power of her presence still shone in her gold-flecked hazel eyes. She sat meekly in the wheelchair, guided by a young male nurse. A tank of oxygen was strapped to the side, and colorless plastic tubes led up to her nostrils. Her hair was gray-streaked and her skin had an unhealthy, livid undertone. She wore a white silk blouse and white slacks that hung on her bony legs. At fifty-four, she was weakened and past her prime years, but her strength and former beauty still lingered in her regal face.

"Did you survive the trip?" asked Ernie, lightly fingering her pulse. "We tried to warn you about the storm when communication was restored, but you had already left."

"We spoke to the authorities on Bali. They said the worst had passed, and there was damage but no danger. I didn't want to waste any time—I don't *have* much time," replied Jana in a deep, wheezing voice. "Where is the wonder healer?"

Madai stepped forward with a small smile.

She studied him intently. "You look weaker than I do," she said brusquely in her hoarse, breathless voice. "You say you've cured cancer?"

"Yes, ma'am."

"Were these people diagnosed by a physician?" she asked. "Some primitive languages use the same word for 'tumor' and 'boil,' so when their native healers claim to cure cancer, they are merely lancing boils."

"We have no laboratory for diagnosis, but Ram went to the hospital on Bali. It was no boil—the tumors look quite different."

"I wonder if you can help me," wheezed Jana tensely. "I'm a sick woman. Part of one lung has already been removed, but the tumor continues to spread. They've tried radiation, chemotherapy, and all their damn, useless quackery. I've spent a fortune but nothing helps. It grows and spreads, stalking me like some horrible curse. I'm terrified of more pain and suffering—and death. It won't go away and soon it will destroy me. No more lungs . . . No more Jana . . . The end. *Can* you help me?"

"If it isn't too far advanced, I can try to destroy it," said Madai.

"Do you think it's too advanced?"

"Maybe not. You're weak and very afraid, but you can still talk and eat and attend to your business."

"I can *feel* myself dying! The slightest exertion makes me gasp and wheeze like a worn-out pipe organ. I dream of oxygen. I crave it like an addict craves drugs. I can feel the pain spreading inside me and I'm desperate. I'll try anything—even witch doctors, and I'm a wealthy woman. You know I'll reward you well if you're successful."

"Yes, ma'am."

"You've made a good impression on my friends, and I trust them. Come onto the boat and we can begin."

Jana's boyish blond nurse, Michael, wheeled her back up the ramp. Ernie, Sonia, and Paul walked alongside, talking in low tones. Madai and Lasmi followed them, hand in hand. Ketut, Dawan, and their parents trailed behind, gazing in silent awe at this lavish wonder of a boat.

To Madai, the interior of the yacht was a fairyland as strange and magical as anything he'd seen with the Moonbird. Jana ordered refreshments to be served in the galley, and while they waited, Michael gave the wide-eyed islanders a tour.

The Chinese store had a rickety petrol-powered generator that produced enough electricity for some dim light globes and a small refrigerator, but this was Madai's first real glimpse of the exciting modern world. He knew of such marvels from the glossy ads in the moldering magazines at the mission library, but now it all came alive for him.

He stared in rapt fascination at a videotaped melodrama, with a confusing plot and blaring music, projected onto a wide, glazed surface. It resembled their island shadow drama, but no tireless dalang sat entranced behind the screen to manipulate the puppets. The actors rushed about with a life of their own, through forces stranger than any Madai had ever seen.

His excitement was boundless when the blond nurse, Michael, showed them the stateroom filled with vital medical equipment from Jana's private jet. He listened to a stethoscope and heard his own heart pumping his blood with tireless rhythm.

Michael showed him X-rays from the portable machine, and Madai saw the actual structure of a human lung in its protective bone cage for the first time. It looked like his sojourns inside the organs—but so impersonal and abstract.

His family was enchanted by the living room and the galley. His mother giggled when she touched the food in the freezer with a tentative hand. Ketut leaped back when the gas stove burst into flame at the touch of a button. Lasmi ran her hands lovingly over the brocade draperies and silky teak wall paneling, and the sleek, comfortable furniture. Dawan glanced shyly at her reflection in a large mirror and sank gingerly into a soft leather sofa. She bounced up and down with a little laugh. Michael sat beside her, his soft blue eyes fixed on her delicate features with a fascination that equaled the islanders'.

Madai's father was especially impressed by the W.C. He flushed the toilet several times with keen interest on his leathery face. "Do they raise fish in this?" he asked.

"I don't think so, Bapak," said Madai.

"But they *could* raise fish. Sometimes we catch fry that are too small to eat, but too large to throw back into the sea. I've always thought I should raise them in a pond until they're large enough to cook. I tried it once, but the water got scummy and they all died. If I had something like this, I could lift out the fish and flush the water regularly. They would grow fat and ready to eat—and I wouldn't have to go out fishing for our supper on stormy days. I could lie around the house carving ebony for tourists, and when I got hungry I'd scoop one out and throw it into a pan. It's a good idea, isn't it Madai? I'd like one of these gadgets. If you heal the woman, maybe she'll give it to you."

When a Balinese crewman explained the use of the toilet to Madai's father, his weathered face flushed, and he barked a short laugh.

Marvels upon marvels. Ketut stretched out with a contented grin on a big, soft bed. Madai's mother shrieked when she felt the hot shower. Madai and Lasmi lingered in the library, switching the bright fluorescent lights on and off, and browsing among the exhilarating shelves of thick, crisp books. Madai wanted to stay on this yacht forever and read every one of these books, for each one offered a new world to explore.

Bapak quickly forgot the toilet as the Balinese crewmen dazzled him with the generators, engines, and sophisticated navigation equipment that powered this monolithic vessel. He climbed up into the glass-enclosed pilothouse to try each button and knob, one by one, with single-minded fascination. The big horns blared, the running lights flicked on and off, and the radios crackled.

Michael demonstrated an air conditioner for Dawan, delighting in her long black hair blowing in the artificial breeze. Then he led her up to the polished teak deck to show her the motorbikes lashed to the cabin wall. "Maybe later I can give you a ride," he said.

Dawan nodded her eager assent, for motorbikes are a rare symbol of power on the island, owned only by haughty government officials and the very rich.

They were all summoned to the galley for coffee, little cakes, and their first thrilling taste of Australian ice cream. Madai savored the icy, fruit-flecked sweetness as it melted on his tongue. So *this* was the modern world.

He felt an exciting new sense of power and vigor. All the ordeals of healing the sick ones had been worth it—if they brought him such magic. He glanced at the frail and frightened Amazon huddled in her wheelchair at the head of the table, gasping for breath as she talked to her friends.

Another ordeal was ahead of him. Soon he must leave these luxuries behind and walk alone into the forest, to summon the Moonbird and enter Jana's lungs—and risk his life again to battle the lethal growth inside her.

20

For the healing of Jana Davids, Madai and his family dressed in their finest holiday clothes. He wore a tan and white batik sarong, carefully folded around his waist and wrapped with a clean white band. Scented garlands hung around his neck.

His mother, Lasmi, and Dawan also wore fine batik sarongs, topped with lacy pastel *kebaya* blouses. Their hair was combed into serpentine coils decked with flowers.

Madai had slept soundly and breakfasted on rice gruel and fruit. He had carefully massaged and manipulated the pulses in Jana's bony wrists to strengthen and relax her. Now he prepared to set off along the storm-damaged pathway, into the forest to summon the Moonbird.

"I've been thinking," said Ernie to Madai. "You complained that the acid of the tumor burns your skin. Why don't you wear a diver's rubber wet suit from the yacht? Sharp scalpels and a heavy-duty flashlight would also make your work go quicker. Even if it's all just imaginary, you'd feel more comfortable for the healing," he added tactfully while he sipped a cool lemonade.

"If you could ride with me, you'd see beyond *imaginary*. Time bends . . . Space dwindles and shifts . . . Everything grows smaller, then larger again," said Madai. Yet he eagerly accepted Ernie's well-meaning new ideas.

When he finally departed alone for the banyan and bamboo grove, he was well armed and carrying the protective black rubber suit and helmet of a diver, which made him feel stronger and more confident as he faced the fearsome battle.

Jana sprawled tensely on the comfortable bed in her teak-paneled, air-conditioned stateroom, breathing hoarsely and surrounded by her anxious circle of friends. Madai's family waited nervously in their compound, busying themselves with household chores, and worrying whether Madai had the stamina to fight the foreign sickness. Even Bapak and Ketut stayed home, uneasily carving ebony masks instead of going out fishing.

Madai walked apprehensively into the forest. A big, pale pig sunning along the muddy pathway snorted encouragement, and the bright yellow parakeets shrieked hopefully from the treetops. He summoned the Moonbird quickly and mounted its shimmering back. They flew over the sleek white yacht and entered the wasted body of the stranger.

To Madai, the lungs looked like hollow clusters of grapes, or bunches of bubbles connected by narrow tubules. But Jana's lungs were unlike anything he'd ever seen. They were slashed and scarred by the surgery and radiation—and they were filthy with tarry chemicals and industrial wastes.

Madai and the Moonbird explored the globules and passageways of her lungs with growing surprise. Some areas looked like pictures of bombed-out cities, all blackened and charred by the techniques of modern healers. Even where the doctors hadn't been, there was an overwhelming quality of blackness. Thick deposits of sooty grime and metallic grit coated the remaining healthy tissues. Oddly colored chemical formations grew in irregular mounds and clusters. The malignant vines grew and twined among them, and snaked along the tarry crusts.

"We can fight the tumor with Dr. Ernie's sharp knives," said Madai. "But what can we do about all this poison? She'll never be able to breathe normally with all the filth inside. I've never seen this before on the island—can we clean it out?"

The Moonbird was doubtful. "If we dislodge anything it might choke her. Better to leave it alone. The foreigners live in sterile surroundings—all their dirt is trapped inside. It makes a fertile soil for the deadly vines, and they won't be so easy to fight even with sharp new blades."

The Moonbird was right. The growths were thick and powerful, with choking acid fumes. They twisted and resisted their destruction like sentient creatures.

"The woman is strong and so is her disease," said the Moonbird as they slashed at the tendrils and destroyed them in their own steaming secretions.

Madai moved carefully but jauntily among the cramped passageways, elated by the power of his new weapons, and the rubber diving suit that prevented the acid from burning him.

He cut and slashed—until he slipped into a cavern filled with slimy tar that sucked at him like greedy quicksand and covered his head. He clawed frantically in the muck, trying to gain a foothold. The tar covered his helmet with disorienting blackness and he couldn't breathe. His chest was bursting, and his mind whirled with terrifying claustrophobia. He was trapped and would drown in the toxic filth inside Jana's lung. He felt himself slipping into bleak unconsciousness.

Then his thrashing hand discovered a narrow tubule coated with chemical slime. Laboriously he pulled himself inside, and found a tiny crawl space where he could wedge his body and feverishly catch his breath. Now he was trapped in this cramped opening. "Moonbird!" he shouted. Would his voice carry through the muck? He waited tensely, then went numb with relief when the searching Garuda finally plucked him from the slippery tubule with its beak.

The beautiful diving suit was covered with sticky filth, and Madai's head pounded with weary pain in the acid fumes, but there was no time to clean up and rest. They cut and hacked at the tumor with the sharp, glittering scalpels, and burned it with the acid. Chop, burn, destroy . . . Chop, burn, destroy. Time twisted and coiled like Lasmi's oiled black hair—until finally the job was done.

His eyes and nose were wet and stinging from the fumes as he climbed onto the Moonbird and rested his throbbing head against the shimmering feathers. The Garuda rose out of the foreign woman's body, and returned him to the forest. They had fought all day and night, and now it was nearly dawn.

"Jana will need a complete workup by oncology specialists at the medical center back home," said Ernie later that morning. "But the portable X-ray machine shows *no* malignant lesions! She's coughed up lots of stuff, her lungs look clear, and they're functioning well. She's in spontaneous remission."

"Do you realize what you've done?" Jana asked Madai as she paced back and forth on the teak deck of the yacht—without her wheelchair or oxygen tank. "You've halted a verified case of cancer. I feel stronger than I have in years and that's a miracle!"

"Yes, ma'am," said Madai. "I'm glad you're feeling better now. But you saw all the dirt on the diving suit. Please try to keep your lungs cleaner so it doesn't come back."

"Yes, yes," she snapped. "I know, I'll try. I'll move to the desert and I won't start smoking again—even though I'm dying for a cigarette. But frankly, Madai, your island is a muddy place. Maybe you —*slipped*—while you were in your trance?"

"We don't have mud like that. The tumor vines like to grow in dirty places," said Madai earnestly.

"Okay, stop preaching," said Jana, standing tall and leathery, gnawing on her fingernails with restless energy as her strength returned. "The main point is that you've *healed* me—that's never been done before."

"I've heard there are other healers in other places—"

"They're all fakes. Do you realize there's an epidemic of cancer running wild in America? What should we *do* with you, Madai? I can reward you with money—more money than you ever imagined. What will you do with it?"

"If I have money, we can buy cement to build strong new docks and irrigation ditches to replace the ones that were destroyed in the storm. If the ditches aren't repaired soon, the rice harvest will be completely lost, and we'll have famine. Mud ditches will be washed away by the monsoon, but cement lasts a long time. There's so much damage from the earthquake and the typhoon. If you give me money I can help repair the island."

"Fine. I'll give you enough money to pave this sandbar with cement. Then I want to introduce you to the smug specialists—and I want you to perform your healings for them. We can build a clinic here and turn this island into a posh tropical health resort. If you can regularly produce cures, you'll become rich and famous, Madai. Wealthy people will come from all over the world to see you. We'll construct a luxury hotel, to provide jobs for the natives. With my backing, we'll rebuild this godforsaken place . . . Maybe you could even afford a pair of pants," said Jana, her hazel eyes glittering with excitement.

"The island doesn't *need* to be paved—and Madai doesn't need foreign pants," growled Bapak.

21

"Would you like a ride?" asked Michael, the golden-haired nurse, smiling at Madai's sister, Dawan, with soft blue eyes.

She laughed gaily and her black eyes met his gaze, then dropped modestly. A green and yellow floral sarong was draped around her slight waist and tied with a green band. A filmy green *kebaya* was worn loosely over her diminutive shoulders. Her black hair was coiled around a red hibiscus flower.

Michael rolled the motorbike down to the dock. Madai, Jana, and the others on the teak deck of the sleek yacht glanced at them with indulgent smiles. They were such a pretty pair; fair, towering Michael and dark, petite Dawan. They watched each other like infatuated puppies.

Dawan fluttered with excitement as she climbed onto the seat behind Michael and clasped his waist with her graceful hands. Only the most powerful men on the island could afford motorbikes, which were all the rage on Bali—though few of the island pathways were passable by bike. This was Dawan's first ride and she was thrilled.

Michael gunned the motor, flicked the cheery lights on and off, beeped the horn, and roared up and down the wooden dock, and the roadway that leads to the Chinese store, the government office and guesthouse, and the mission school. A crowd of ragged children ran and shouted after them. Back and forth they tore, faster and faster. The wind whipped her coiled hair, loosening it into long black streamers that flared behind her. The red flower was tossed to the muddy roadside. The sense of speed elated Dawan. She was filled with lively joy as they raced along—faster and faster.

Until the edge of her sarong caught in the rear wheel and pulled her sideways, tipping the bike so it spilled onto her. Michael leaped with feline ease off the falling bike. He landed lithely on his feet, but Dawan wasn't so lucky. Her sarong tangled in the spokes of the wheel, and the weight of the bike landed directly on her. A shower of sparks flew from the engine. The gas tank burst open—and ignited in a great puffball of roaring flame.

Madai and the others on the yacht raced down the dock and the rutted dirt road. His sister's charred, lifeless body lay pinned beneath the wreckage of the bike. Michael stared ahead in a shocked daze.

Madai whipped the moonstone carving from the silver amulet around his neck, and the Moonbird appeared in a startling instant.

"He's gone into a trance," Madai heard Sonia say as they entered Dawan's body with a sharp snap of wings. Inside they found a horrifying scene. It looked like a bomb had exploded, leaving ruined shards and fragments of smoking debris.

"There's no way to fight this, nothing we can do for her," said Madai numbly as tears poured down his angular cheeks. They moved sorrowfully among the blasted ruins of Dawan's body.

She wasn't entirely gone, for some nerves were still intact and firing in random patterns. They hurried up to her brain to see if any consciousness remained. Large portions were burned out, yet certain parts of her mind were unharmed—still alive, and as they flashed on and off in irregular cerebral patterns, Madai could detect faint images.

He saw the image of a small, black-haired girl marching purposefully into the forest, with her little brother, Madai, on her hip, to collect baskets of passion fruit with her friends. He could see the little girl making coco-milk with her gap-toothed mother in the sun-dappled courtyard of their wicker compound.

He saw her collecting eggs one morning from an irate hen that flapped its wings, squawked, pecked at her face, and frightened her. He could see her nodding with sleepy boredom at the mission school on a hot afternoon.

He saw her winding soft cotton cloth around her hair, to carry a big bundle of laundry to the pond, walking straight and proud, and carefully balancing the burden on her head. At the placid green pond, Dawan, Lasmi, and the other girls cleaned the clothes on the rocks, bathed among pink lotuses, and gossiped about the pesky boys of the desa while blue dragonflies gossiped overhead.

He could see her sitting sadly beside Madai's sleeping mat, his scalp and body covered with wounds after the terrible healing of Ram. She'd been so devoted to him that she'd never married, and he could feel her sorrow.

Madai's tears flowed faster.

He wandered sobbing among the haphazard images and memories, feelings and sensations of Dawan's dying brain. "Save her, Moonbird!" he cried. "She's still alive—do something to *save* her."

"Nothing can be done," whispered the Moonbird.

Gradually the images flickered out as her brain continued to die, bit by bit. Then there was nothing but darkness.

"*Beh!* Save her, Moonbird."

"She's dead," whispered the Garuda.

"Do *something!*"

"There's nothing to do."

"Then what good are you? We heal everyone on the island and even foreigners—but you won't help me when I need you. You *must* know some god trick. You could heal her if you tried—why won't you even *try?*" Madai shook with grief and rage.

"You sound like all the sick ones waiting outside your gate. You know we can't help everyone."

"Try, you overgrown chicken, *try!*" shouted Madai, pounding at the Moonbird's glowing wings with his fists.

"I'm sorry, there's nothing to try. Let me take you back." The Moonbird plucked Madai from his sister's seared body with its beak, and deposited the weeping healer on the roadside.

Madai opened his sunken black eyes and looked around. Dr. Ernie shook his head sadly as he examined Dawan's corpse, and the others were gathered mournfully around the wreckage.

Michael's blue eyes met Madai's, and they stared at each other with profound horror. A flickering halo of pale blue light formed around the tall, fair nurse, blending with Michael's frightened blue eyes.

Over his head appeared the shard of Rangda, in a subliminal flash of blue. With one cold, malevolent eye, a tusked cheek, a tangle of copper hair, and her mouth fixed in a sneer. "Shall we *see* him, my son?" hissed the shard of Rangda in Madai's mind.

"*Yes!*" he cried silently, still frantic with sorrow and rage. "See him. If he wants speed—give him *speed!*"

The shard of Rangda laughed, and flashed and darted among the treetops. The nimbus of blue around Michael began to pulse. Faster and faster, with ever-increasing tempo, until the strobelike flicker grew too rapid for Madai's eyes.

"See," hissed Rangda, swooping above them. "*See him* . . ."

Then all of Michael's cellular processes began to accelerate—and Michael began to visibly age as Madai and the others stared, aghast. Fine lines appeared on his face, and his golden hair was streaked with gray. His torso began to stoop and his robust muscles shriveled. Before everyone's eyes, Michael became a man of late middle age. He looked around with an uncertain smile, and walked toward Madai with imploring hands extended.

"*See,*" hissed Rangda, soaring kitelike among the clouds.

The eerie blue flicker whirled around him with increasing velocity, and Michael grew even older. His hair thinned to wisps of jaundiced white. His runny eyes were filmed with cataracts, and wiry hair sprouted in his ears and nostrils. His skin was crinkled tissue paper, with knotted blue veins and discolored blotches. He tried to speak, but his mouth opened vacantly and his teeth fell to the mud. His back was bent, his chest sunken, and his hands gnarled with arthritis. He barked with pain as his inner organs began to decay.

"*See* him . . ."

Michael was now a senile old man with a confused and withered face. He chuckled mindlessly. Then he wet his pants, glanced down with surprise, and took one step forward. He clutched his chest as his worn heart thumped erratically and failed. Michael collapsed in the rutted dirt road, a deceased elder of twenty-six, beside a burned-out motorbike and a dead native girl.

Rangda laughed shrilly above him as the flashing blue faded away.

Dawan and Michael had flown like butterflies to wait on the far shore . . .

Madai looked around defiantly. The others all stared at him with terrified eyes. Except Jana Davids, who wore an odd little smile—which somehow reminded him of the smile of Rangda.

"Yes, I *see* . . ." stammered Jana, her hazel eyes looking glazed.

IV

Madai quarreled with the Moonbird . . .

22

Madai raced down the pathway into the forest, his face twisted with terror.

"See . . . See . . . *See* . . ." echoed the hiss of Rangda from the treetops.

"He seeeess," mimicked a swarm of stinging gnats.

He ran blindly until he reached the storm-shattered grove of banyans and bamboos. There he stopped, panting and sobbing, and held the moonstone image of the Garuda to the dappled sunlight.

"Why did you let her die?" he wept. "You could have saved her if you *tried*. Why wouldn't you try?"

The banyan tree sighed.

"How could you abandon me to the power of Rangda? You know I can't fight the Antagonist alone. You first showed me the witch's ugly face—long ago on the lantern ship. I never *asked* to see it. I never asked for *any* of this. You appeared one day to give me powers, and revealed the face of the evil one. Now you won't help me when I need you—and Rangda wants me for her own. *You* brought the malignant power of the witch to me."

The clearing was strangely silent. Madai was caught in an undertow of mindless frustration and rage.

"Why did you let her die, you damn chicken, *why?*" he cried, beating the moonstone image furiously against a sharp rock—and chipping off part of the beak. Madai stared, aghast, at the broken image in his hand. "Moonbird!" he called forlornly. "Where are you, Moonbird?"

After a long moment the Moonbird appeared, but it was no longer the strong and shimmering Garuda that Madai had always known. Now the Moonbird looked small and weak and cloudy—an insubstantial phantasm of tissue paper—with a shattered beak.

"You're a grown man now," came the faint, rustling whisper in his mind. "You're no longer a light-minded boy who can ride upon my back. I don't live in your world of time. I hadn't noticed how much you'd grown. You're a man now, with the anger and appetites of an adult. Your flesh has grown dense and solid, and I can no longer carry you."

"But what about the healings? All the sick ones will die!"

"It is the nature of ailing things to die. Decay is inherent in all components, and whatever has form must founder."

"That's not true! When we fly inside the bodies they sometimes *do* survive. It's your duty to help me battle the witch. You *must* carry me."

"You are fully grown and solid now. You can never become a light-minded boy again." The Garuda's voice sounded very far away. "It is illusion to think so and illusion is not real . . . *Not real* . . ." The words echoed in the air, then ebbed and were gone.

"Stop saying that! Just because I grew angry doesn't mean I've entirely changed. I'll grow light again, I promise. You can carry me if you *try* . . ."

Madai leaped toward the vague and tissuey Moonbird and tried to clamber upon its back. But the cloudy, insubstantial figure crumpled under his weight, faded, and disappeared.

"Moonbird!" cried Madai. "Please come back, Moonbird."

But there was no answer. When Madai held the chipped moonstone image up to the light, it looked dull, dark, and opaque. The Moonbird had lost its inner glow.

"*Moonbird!*" called Madai, terrified. "Where are you?"

But the broken moonstone image remained silent—and the Moonbird was gone.

Madai waited and stormed at the lifeless stone figure as dreary clouds gathered overhead, and a drizzle slipped among the trees.

"It isn't just . . . You have the feelings of an arrogant stone idol. What will they all say when they learn that I've lost my powers? Please come back . . . What will I *do?*"

The dullness of the sky echoed the dullness of the moonstone, and the dull patter of rain on the leaves. P'tat, p'tat . . . Puddles collected at Madai's feet, and the droning of gnats and mosquitoes had a mocking song. He couldn't stay in the forest, yet how could he return to the desa on that dreadful, drizzly day?

What would his family and the foreigners say about the death of Michael and his failure to save Dawan? What would they do when they learned that the Moonbird had left him? Madai was overcome with shame.

But had he *really* lost his healing powers? The foreigners had told him again and again that the Moonbird was superstitious nonsense, a figment of his imagination, a fantasy invented as a child to explain his powers to himself. According to the learned doctors, the healing gift didn't come from the Garuda, it came from deep inside Madai himself. Well, he was no longer a child. Even the Moonbird had told him that. Perhaps he no longer needed childish fantasies. *"Put away childish things,"* as Father Hans quoted from the prophet Paul. Maybe he could concentrate and do the healings alone, and save many lives to atone for the deaths of Michael and Dawan.

Madai spent the rest of that gloomy day in the forest, concentrating on wisps of fog, and going through the motions of a healing trance. He tried to imagine entering a sick baby in the desa, and fighting the germbugs. He tried to focus as hard as he could, but nothing happened . . . Nothing at all. The real world of the rain forest refused to fade, and Madai knew that the child still ailed.

Now he must languish in a steamy boat, and drink beer with the fishermen all day—when there *was* beer to drink. It seemed impossible. How could he lose his powers so quickly? Madai sat in the drizzle and stared at the dull, opaque image, and prayed that it would glow again. But the stone remained dark and the Moonbird wouldn't reappear. As though sung by all the insects, the Garuda's words repeated themselves. "It is not real . . . *Not real* . . ."

Madai's head ached and his eyes burned. Finally he stole apprehensively back to the desa. He wanted someplace peaceful and silent to rest and think. He wouldn't mention the loss of the Moonbird to anyone—not yet. Too much had already happened, and it was better to let everyone calm down. Later he'd tell them his powers were gone.

It was all the excitement brought by the foreigners that had upset his mind, and killed Dawan, and made the Moonbird angry with him. Perhaps the Garuda would return if the strangers went away. Maybe a quiet life would make him light again, so he could fly the Moonbird.

Then a face appeared, hovering in the drizzly mists of the pathway. It was the flickering shard of Rangda, with one eye and tufts of tangled copper hair. The shard of Rangda smiled at him through the blue mist—a smile that somehow reminded him of Jana Davids.

"You haven't lost *all* your powers, my son," hissed the shard of Rangda. "You still have powers to *see* . . ."

Now it was Madai's turn to murmur, "It is not real . . . *Not real* . . ." But alas, in his heart he *did* believe that this illusion was real.

23

At the desa there was no chance to rest, because preparations were already under way for Dawan's death rites and cremation. Michael's remains would be quickly and quietly cremated and sent home.

All the people of the local communities were bustling in and out of Madai's family compound. The men wore white bands of mourning wrapped around their heads. Yet sorrow had already merged into celebration, for Dawan's soul had been freed from its earthly bonds, and would embark on a great journey to join the ancestors in the realm of light-without-shadow. There her spirit would linger until it was reborn into the family in a new human form. Thus the family is related in an endless cycle. Great-granny is reborn as her own grandchild.

Dawan's body had been cleaned and laid out in the courtyard. The white-robed village priest chanted and mumbled as he blessed her, and put bits of broken mirrors on her closed eyelids. Flecks of mica were sprinkled onto her limbs to give her light and strength in the next world. A moonstone was placed in her mouth for wisdom; spices and fragrant flowers were spread over her body; and she was wrapped in a white shroud.

Neighbors filed in to say their farewells, carrying pots of spicy fish curry, skewers of grilled chicken, fried noodles, and other refreshments and offerings, which they heaped in the courtyard. Tomorrow Dawan would be temporarily buried in the village graveyard while the priests consulted astrological texts inscribed on palm bark, to decide an auspicious date for the cremation ceremony.

The three foreigners waited for Madai too. Ernie absently peeled and ate tiny sweet bananas from a large stem that lay nearby. He patted Madai's thin shoulder sympathetically with a large, gentle hand.

"Terribly sorry about your sister," said Paul. "Jana sends her condolences, and she wants to talk to you. She still isn't strong enough to hike to the village, so she asked you to come at once to the yacht."

"It's nearly dark and it's raining," said Madai reluctantly. "Tell her I'll come tomorrow."

"She says it's important. *Please* come now."

Madai uneasily followed the subdued foreigners back to the dock, where the lights of the yacht blazed cheerily in the dusky drizzle. Now the sleek vessel held no magic for Madai, for its arrival had brought death to Dawan.

They found Jana, tall and leathery, restlessly drinking bourbon and ice in the lounge. "You *caused* it, didn't you Madai?" she demanded as they entered. "You somehow caused Michael's death."

"Not purposely," said Madai defensively.

"You can heal—and you can *kill*," she continued, her gold-flecked eyes wide and bright. "How do you do it?"

"I . . . don't know," stammered Madai. "*Rangda* did it."

"What is Rangda?"

"Rangda is a spirit like the Moonbird, but very ugly and evil. Sometimes the witch comes to me instead of the Moonbird. Now only part of her comes—because Doctor Sonia broke her mask. Everyone on the island is afraid of Rangda. Whenever she appears, something terrible happens. When she comes to me I see dreadful visions—but I don't *cause* bad things—Rangda does."

"I *see* . . . You're a very strange fellow, Madai, and very naive," said Jana. "You say that spirits come to you. Good, beautiful spirits that make people well, and evil, ugly spirits that make them ill. Don't you realize that *both* spirits are aspects of your own mind? They aren't *real*, Madai. They're figments that you invented when you were a boy to explain your strange powers. You still can't accept that *you* cure disease—or cause it. You cling to your childish phantasms as if they were real, because you're afraid to confront your own strength. No one can see these imaginary playmates except you —because it *is* you. *You* healed me, not some flashy cockatoo! *You* saw Michael with the evil eye, not some wicked witch."

"No!" shouted Madai. "It's not true. I don't have such awful powers. *I* didn't kill Michael, Rangda did."

"Has this ever happened before?" asked Jana, adding more bourbon to the ice cubes in her glass.

"Maybe once . . ." admitted Madai.

"When?"

"Rangda saw the widower Ram . . . and he got stomach cancer. I healed him, and that's when I became bald."

"I *see* . . . Were you angry with Ram?" asked Jana.

"A little. He wanted to marry Lasmi."

"She's your fiancée, so you must have been *very* angry."

"A *little,*" repeated Madai sullenly.

"You were angry with Ram and he became seriously ill. You were angry with Michael and he dropped dead. Do you need more proof? You can cure—and kill. You're a *very* powerful man."

"I tell you, it's Rangda!"

"Suit yourself," said Jana with a breathy little laugh. "I don't want your angry eyes to see *me!*"

"You're afraid of me, aren't you?" asked Madai. "You think I'm an evil man who should be punished."

"No, I'm not afraid of you," smiled Jana. "I *admire* you. You're not evil—you're strong. I don't want to punish you, I want to take you back with me—to America. You'll perform your healings there and become frightfully rich, and see the exciting modern world that fascinates you so. If you want, I'll send you to medical school so you'll know both Western and native medicine. We'll set up a clinic and you'll do quite well. Your girlfriend can come along too."

"*America!*" breathed Madai, quite taken by surprise.

"That's right," laughed Jana. "You look like a young Yul Brynner—they'll *love* you there. I'll cover all your expenses until you get established, but I want you to do two things for me."

"What's that?" asked Madai suspiciously.

"First, I want you to keep me alive as long as possible, and keep the damn tumor away. I'm terrified that it will recur. Secondly, I have some enemies. *Nasty* men; I know you'll be furious when I tell you about them. I want your wicked witch to *see* them for me."

"Jana!" interrupted Sonia, staring at the older woman with shocked brown eyes. "Has some evil spirit possessed *you?*"

"Don't *Jana* me!" she snorted, downing her drink. "You weren't squeamish about my business when you accepted my research grants. You know I'm a ruthless old gargoyle. Now leave us alone."

"This is different . . . You can't *buy* Madai . . ." said Ernie with a frown as he reluctantly left the lounge with Sonia and Paul.

"You mean you want Rangda to *kill* your enemies?" asked Madai hesitantly.

"You can *see* it that way if you want. But it would be our undetectable little secret, wouldn't it?" smiled Jana, her hazel eyes flickering feverishly. "There must be some reason why you were blessed with both powers. There are many wicked people who should be destroyed—that's doing good too. Your life is changing and your powers are shifting. That's normal and there's no reason to worry. Your strength is at its height, so take advantage of it. You'll destroy evil people just as you destroy evil disease. Both powers are gifts—so use them!"

". . . I don't know," said Madai, feeling frightened.

"Well, think about it and let me know tomorrow morning. You need time to get used to the idea, and you'll *see* that it's a real opportunity for you. I can't lounge around this sandbar too long. I'll sail back to Bali tomorrow, and we'll take care of all the immigration formalities there. Think about life in *America*."

24

Madai didn't return to his family compound that night. He knew sleep would be impossible with the noisy preparations for Dawan's funeral, and the whirling confusion in his mind. He followed the beam of his flashlight to the soothing calm of the crumbling village temple, and rested in the verdant courtyard with the crickets and melancholy nightbirds.

America! She would whisk him to fabled America—Lasmi too. They would ride in airplanes and big, shiny cars, and see roads as wide as the Waringan River. They'd ride lifts in buildings that scrape the sky, and see the cinema. Maybe they could visit Disneyland, where rockets fly to the moon. The whole modern world would come to life for them!

If he would keep Jana alive—and kill her enemies. Unthinkable. He could never aid her evil schemes, and he had no more power to keep her alive. Yet this was his only chance to see America.

Maybe he should cheat her. He could claim that both the Moonbird and Rangda had abandoned him in America, and that all his powers were gone. She'd grow angry and send them home, but meanwhile they'd see many extraordinary things.

Perhaps that was the answer. Trick Jana Davids and gain revenge for Dawan.

A blue flare shot across the sky like a meteor and interrupted his thoughts. He looked up and the blue light overhead resolved into the leering shard of Rangda.

"You haven't lost *all* your powers," she hissed. "You still have powers to *see*. Rangda never tells you how to live, my son. She wants you to pursue pleasures. Seeing makes you so strong, my son . . . See . . ."

Warily Madai tried to ignore the eerie shard of Rangda, but the witch seemed to grow increasingly powerful without the Moonbird to keep her at bay.

The shard of Rangda flashed everywhere, with a pulsing effect that created a throbbing ache behind his eyes. Rangda was in the black sky and on the mossy temple walls, among the scented treetops and the thatched pagoda towers. Wherever Madai looked he saw Rangda, beating like a heart and growing ever stronger.

"See what's best to see," hissed Rangda. The shard of the witch stared at him with one cold eye, her coppery hair hung in matted tangles, and her white tusked mouth was fixed in a sneer. The night air felt desolate and cold as Madai paced in the temple courtyard, trying to stay warm and calm as the Antagonist pulsed all around him.

"See what you can *see*, my son," hissed Rangda.

And Madai saw more wealth and power—and death than he'd ever imagined. He envisioned himself standing on the iron balcony of a grand stone mansion. Lasmi stood beside him, caressing his body and tending to his needs.

He stood on the balcony of his great mansion in America and stared with eyes of black steel. And wherever he stared, wailing people fell, overcome with weakness and pain. Madai stood tall and firm, and stared at Jana's enemies. They fell to the ground, groaning as death raced through their bodies.

"*See*," hissed Rangda.

Madai stood on his balcony, caressed by Lasmi, and stared with glittering eyes of steel. He could stare at anyone—anywhere—and watch them sicken and die. His power had no limit, but Madai wasn't cruel. No. *He* wouldn't destroy randomly. He'd only stare with stern metallic eyes at the wicked ones who deserved to die. Jana would show him her enemies, but Madai would make the final decision. Who would live and who would die—like a vengeful god.

He'd gain wealth and power and pleasure beyond measure. Everyone would fear and obey him, lest he stare at them with steely eyes. Jana and all the learned doctors would speak to him with deference and respect. Finally they would believe that his powers were *real*.

But he wouldn't kill for petty reasons. He would do good, as he'd done as a healer, exterminating the wicked and heartless ones who live on human prey.

When he was a boy, he'd wondered why creatures were divided into the eaten and the eaters. Now he would become one of the eaters.

"See them, my son," hissed Rangda, throbbing everywhere.

Madai paced feverishly in the icy bleakness of the night, then entered the main temple pagoda, trying to elude the grasping shard. "I can't do it," he whispered . . . "It's *wrong*."

"It's *easy!*" laughed Rangda from her wicker hut on the altar. "You'll be so *strong*. You can marry Lasmi . . . See how satisfied you can be . . ."

Madai wandered deliriously around the quake-damaged temple complex, stumbling among the shadowy thatched pagodas and dance pavilions, the mossy icons and sweet flowering shrubs. He saw none of them. All he could see was the laughing shard, urging him to do horrible things.

He was terrified by Rangda, and by the seductive vision of metal-eyed Madai on that black iron balcony, living in luxury and possessing the power of life and death. He knew it was wrong to let the witch take and tempt him—as she had apparently taken and tempted Jana's mind. *Fearfully* wrong. Where would the path of death ultimately lead? Yet if he cooperated with Jana and Rangda to kill at their command, this mighty life could be his.

And if he *didn't* cooperate, then what? Now that the Moonbird was gone, he'd be exposed as a failure or a fake. There'd be no more throngs of people begging to see Madai. No more grateful families thanking him with loving gifts. No more scientists eager to talk to him.

He'd eke out a dull livelihood catching fish and spawning—like a normal man.

Where was the Moonbird? Madai glanced at the lifeless stone image and felt a rush of anger. Why had the Moonbird abandoned him and allowed this to happen? Surely the Garuda could forgive him! When the Moonbird was with him, Rangda's menacing presence remained in the background. As long as Madai could heal, he couldn't be tempted by dark powers. *Why* wouldn't the Moonbird return to help the sick ones, and save him from being overwhelmed by the malevolent possession of the witch?

"Moonbird!" Madai called feebly into the icy wind.

There was no answer . . . There was no answer. There was only the dreadful flicker of Rangda urging him to kill. Had he actually killed before? Was *he* directly responsible for Ram's tumor and Michael's eerie death? He'd never consciously tried to harm them, though he'd felt great anger toward both of them. He'd always insisted that Rangda was at fault, but was it Rangda alone—or Madai acting through the witch?

Now it would be different. If Madai chose the path of evil, there'd be no doubt that he'd deliberately cause suffering and death. He knew it was wicked and wrong. All the priests, teachers, and villagers would say it was wrong. Lasmi and his family, and all the unfortunates who trusted him, would say it was wrong. Yet now that his healing gift was gone, he would sink into dull obscurity on the island.

He never really wanted that. He *enjoyed* having power. Now Jana and Rangda were offering him ultimate power. But he needn't be limited by Jana's fevered demands. He could gaze with eyes of dark steel at anyone who angered him; anyone who was cruel or harmful and shouldn't live. He'd destroy the human vermin. He could gaze with cold, ferrous eyes at tyrants and murderers and warmongers. Thus he could atone for his crimes by doing good. This was a temptation that Madai couldn't ignore.

"See what's best to see, my son . . ." hissed Rangda.

"Yes, I *see* . . ." stammered Madai.

Something moved in the black shadows of the sandstone temple wall. Moved swiftly. Four lithe, swarthy men in loincloths slipped from behind the shrubbery and surrounded Madai. Their faces and matted, frizzy hair were painted with streaks of colored mud. They carried long kris daggers, with wavy blades, which they pointed directly at him.

"*Beh!*" cried Madai.

"You come with us, healer-man," said one, in the pidgin dialect of the mountain tribes.

More men leaped from the shadows. Madai had a confused impression of a dark and wild-looking gang, shorter and stockier than the slim and graceful people of the desas. They smelled of strange oils and were tattooed in weird patterns. They wore loincloths and ragtag khakis that must have been scavenged from government soldiers long ago.

Rough, calloused hands seized him. Strong arms lifted him up and carried him through the bush, slashing their way with sharp machetes that sliced easily through the toughest vines. Sweaty arms bore him away from the temple and the shard of Rangda, into the hillsides above the neat orchards and terraced rice paddies. Into the wild mountain valleys where leopards, apes, and warthogs lurk, and where the tribal bands of the First-Ones build flimsy thatched villages along overgrown creeks.

"Flee!" screamed an amber-eyed owl. But there was no way that Madai could flee from these fierce men and their keen blades.

He heard the rhythmic heartbeat of drums, and saw mud-painted bodies in motion near the campfire. He heard babies squalling in ramshackle palm-thatch shelters.

Madai had sometimes seen shy bands of the primitive First-Ones, when they came down from the hills to sullenly trade monkey furs, parrot feathers, and mountain yams and herbs. But nobody from the settled and orderly desas along the Waringan River dared venture into the hidden glens where the First-Ones dwell.

Swarthy arms unceremoniously dumped Madai near a campfire that shot sparks into the mountain breeze. He heard drums and strange babble, and smelled the charred odor of hastily cooked meat. An old man with tangled silver hair and a thin beard was wrapped in a ragged cloth. He lay near the fire, tended by leathery, bare-chested women wearing bone nose rings, and threadbare sarongs tucked loosely around their waists.

The leader of the kidnappers pointed his glittering, sinuous dagger toward the silver-haired figure and said, "Raja dying. You fix my father, healer-man, or my kris fix *you*."

"My son is rude," apologized the reclining elder with a thin, reedy voice. "He never learned the refined manners of the proud lowland river folk. I studied your speech and your ways when I was a lad, working as a bearer for the red-faced Dutch. I'm no longer a lad . . . I'm very old and weak. The endless night of death hovers before my eyes. Our traders brought word that you can revive the dead, so my sons plotted to bring you here. Is it true, healer-man? Can you bring the light back into my eyes?"

"No, Bapak. I wish I could outwit death," said Madai, staring into the fire with a long sigh. "Your traders bring false rumors. Once I could heal sickness such as fevers and worms, but I cannot fan the flame of life beyond its natural time."

It was the old aboriginal chief's turn to sigh. "I feared it would be so, for I see that you are a man, not a god—and a puny man, to speak honestly. Now my sons will be reluctant to free you, for they're afraid that you'll call your men and the government soldiers to take our hidden village. Yet we are peaceable folk; surely you know that. We have always lived on this island, which we did not name, for it was our entire world. My mothers welcomed your lordly race when they fled the clan wars on Bali in their fish-headed boats. Our Raja of those dimly remembered days shared our land with your fathers, in return for sharp daggers, and goods and knowledge from beyond our coral reef. Our mothers gave your people the marshy, mosquito-ridden river valley, for we don't cultivate your rice. We kept the hilly forests for ourselves, for we have always been mountain hunters. We welcomed your people, but they pursued us like animals with their beaters and krises, and pushed us farther and farther back into the hills. We welcomed the long-nosed, sunburned Dutchmen, big and hairy as russet orangutans. We rarely raided their storehouses, even when they stole our strongest men to work as slaves in the clove plantations." The old Raja coughed weakly.

Then he continued in a feeble voice as reminiscences flooded his mind. "The splendid aristocrats of Bali marched to their death rather than submit to the sandy-haired Hollanders. In the Dutch year of 1906, the Balinese nobles burned their sculpted palaces to the ground, and marched in formation in gilded ceremonial finery, chanting their own funeral song. They lifted their jeweled krises, still singing, as Dutch rifles stained the beaches with their proud royal blood. Four thousand men, women, and children of Bali died on that terrible day. *My* people submitted and we survived, but terribly weakened. We submitted to the rifles of the quick little Japanese, who marched like ants in wilted uniforms across our island, then marched away and disappeared. We submitted to the gruff soldiers from Java, who carried deadly machine guns and the Koran. They tried to conscript our men to build roads into the mountains, but the roads were never built, for we slipped away, farther into the wilderness, apart from other men who seek to rule us. We are the First-Ones. This island is ours because we have always lived here. Now my sons fear that I will soon die, and my knowledge of our people will die with me. That's why they brought you here, for they feel sorrow that our race must perish. Old men—and old races—cannot live beyond their time. You say that you cannot lift the hand of death from my eyes, that you only heal fevers and worms. When my sons see that you've failed, they'll grow angry and kill you—rather than let you lead the soldiers to our camp."

Madai listened politely as the old aboriginal chief rambled on in the fluttering glow of the campfire. "I won't lead soldiers here, Bapak," he reassured the elder. "Let me go and I'll keep your secret safely."

"Some of our babies are burning with fevers. If you cool them, you'll win my sons' trust—then they'll free you." The shrewd old chief had made his counteroffer.

"But I no longer have the power even to cool fevers . . ." Madai tried to explain.

The silver-haired old man stared at Madai for a long moment. "Why not, lad? Do I see trouble in your eyes?"

Madai began to talk. He told the old chief about the Moonbird—and Rangda. It felt strangely good to unburden himself to this uncomplicated but wise elder, who didn't scoff with sophisticated words like "figment."

"I know of the witch, she has plagued our people too," nodded the dying chief.

Madai spoke of his love for Lasmi and the perilous healing of Ram. He told about the arrival of the foreigners, and the deaths of Michael and Dawan. Finally, under the old Raja's probing gaze, he revealed the eerie alliance between Jana and Rangda, and the tempting visions of wealth and power in America.

The dimming eyes of the aboriginal chief glittered with anger. *"You must drive the foreigners away!* Even when they wear smiles, they bring trouble to the peoples of the island. They've already killed your sister, now the woman has been invaded by the Sorceress, and wants to kill more. They are messengers of death, and the witch feeds on their wickedness and grows stronger—then turns the weak foreign minds to vicious thoughts. The strangers drove the gentle Garuda away, and barter power with Rangda! Banish the foreigners and the witch will grow quiet again. Believe me, lad, for I have lived many years and seen many strangers come to our island. Some offer friendship, some carry weapons, but sorrow always travels with them. Marry your woman and rest in her arms. It's right for a man to have children to lean on when he grows old and feeble. Perhaps someday the Garuda will return, and you can fly to our mountain village to heal the babies of fevers and worms—but first you must send the strangers away!" The old chief lay back, pale and breathless from the effort of speaking so long.

"I think you're right, Bapak," said Madai slowly.

26

"The First-Ones *stole* Madai," reported Ketut. "I was worried about my brother, so I followed him from the dock after he talked to the foreign woman. He was so upset about Dawan's death that I feared he might do himself harm. He went to the temple, where he paced and mumbled, almost in a trance. Then a band of First-Ones jumped from the bushes. They were covered with mud and tattoos, and had big, sharp krises . . . and they carried Madai away with them."

"Most unusual," said Father Hans, the affable mission priest. Ketut and Lasmi sat uncomfortably on tall chairs in the airy, rattan-furnished parlor of the Catholic mission, which was a simple, white-washed wooden building with a sloping red tin roof, topped by a prettily carved jackwood cross. A breeze blew through the wicker-slatted windows and old lace curtains, and brought the scent of flowers from Father Hans' beloved horticultural garden.

"Who are these First-Ones?" frowned the New Zealander, Paul Robbes, who had come to the mission to fret about the missing healer—for he was also worried after Madai's last encounter with Jana.

"The Republic of Indonesia is a chop suey of ethnic groups and religions," said balding, rotund Father Hans. "My own father was an old-fashioned Dutch colonial, and my mother was a Catholic convert from the island of Flores. The Javanese Muslims are the largest single group, but we have many Chinese, Hindus, Christians, and aborigines—all blended together by *adat*, which are the ancient, unwritten customs of the islands. The First-Ones are thought to be of Malay stock—when they are thought of at all. They were pushed out of Southeast Asia thousands of years ago, and established their matrilineal hunting and gathering communities on isolated islands of the Indonesian archipelago. Nobody even pretends to remember their original name or history, but the dim legends say they were fierce headhunters and cannibals. They cling to their primitive ways, but successive waves of invasion have weakened and depopulated them, and have driven them into retreat in the remote mountain forests. There they live quietly, hunting monkeys and other game, growing a dreadful-tasting white yam, and avoiding civilization, whether it comes from Hindus, Dutch, or Muslims." Father Hans paused to sip Chinese tea from a delftware cup, and to bite into a sugary biscuit.

"On our island, an exiled clan of rebellious Brahmans from Bali became the dominant group some centuries ago. Their descendants are the Hindu peasants of the communal desas along the Waringan River Valley. They have lived peaceably with the First-Ones for a long time, bartering rice for forest products, and avoiding conflict— and each other."

"Then why did they take Madai?" asked Paul.

"I've sent my houseboys to snoop around," said Father Hans. "They brought back word that the old Raja of the First-Ones is dying. Perhaps they took Madai to their village to heal him."

"Let's report this to the government police office down near the dock," said Paul.

"I think not," smiled Father Hans, wiping his shiny pink pate. "The First-Ones aren't fond of soldiers with guns, and they might be provoked to harm Madai. I'd advise doing nothing right now. Perhaps Madai will cure their old chief, and the tribesmen will carry him home as a hero, laden with monkey skins and gifts. I'd let the slow workings of the traditional island laws of *adat* take their leisurely course."

"But we don't have *time* to wait—Jana wants to go back to Bali," said Paul.

Father Hans shrugged. "Time has very little meaning on these islands."

Lasmi looked around the parlor, at the big ebony Jesus hanging on an ornate crucifix; at the billowy portrait of Mother Mary cradling the gaunt body of her slain son; at the faded print of haloed Saint Sebastian gazing heavenward while arrows pierced his pale flesh. Lasmi had always wondered why the kindly gods of the mission were usually depicted as dead.

At dawn the ramshackle village was ominously silent, for the silver-haired Raja of the First-Ones was dead. A shrunken and tattooed old shamaness with a monkey bone in her nose chanted in a thin, singsong voice, and burned herbs to bring back his spirit. But it had already flown to the mountains of darkness and would never return.

"You bring him back, healer-man," insisted the Raja's eldest son.

"*I can't,*" repeated Madai, whose ankle was tied to a tree by a tight leather thong, and who grew increasingly frightened for his life.

"Then you will join my father," said the swarthy, mud-painted warrior, fingering his kris with a menacing glower.

Faintly Madai heard a strange sound pulsing in the forest, blending with the rhythmic throb of the old shamaness's ceremonial bone rattle. The odd sound grew louder until it resolved into a distant *chak . . . chak . . . chak!*

The monkey troop burst into the treetops, following their white, clip-tailed leader. Whooping and chakking, they threw bristly cones from the upland pines at the startled tribe.

"What's *this!*" cried the Raja's son. "Monkey meat!"

The stocky, frizzy-haired men of the village leaped into action, grabbing sharply pointed stones from a pile near the campfire, and flinging them at the monkeys with deadly aim. A russet-furred ape was struck in the head, and fell screaming from the branches of a tall pine. The men rushed forward to slay the thrashing animal with their lethal krises.

In the commotion, the white monkey swung down from the branches and landed with a thud near Madai. He began to gnaw through the leather thong that bound Madai's leg, but the Raja's son spotted him and raced toward them, shouting, with his dagger raised high.

"*Run!*" shouted Madai. "They'll kill you."

At that moment the white monkey severed the leather thong, and scooped Madai in a sinewy, coarse-furred arm. Together they scooted up into the tree, but the Raja's enraged son followed them, bellowing curses, his serpentine dagger glowing in the misty light.

They climbed into the highest branches, with the Raja's son close behind. Madai wasn't used to such dizzy heights without the comforting presence of the Moonbird, and the sunlight glared in his eyes, making it hard to see. The Raja's matted-haired son was nearly upon them, and Madai clung to a precarious crook between a thin branch and the trunk while the white monkey turned back, unarmed, to face their foe.

The swarthy tribal warrior had one arm wrapped around a thick branch, and his legs were wedged in a nook where two branches joined. His free hand held the dagger, and his eyes shot fury. The white monkey squatted almost nonchalantly before him and toyed with a pinecone. The panting warrior lunged forward with his upraised kris, and the white monkey sprang backward. The warrior lunged again, and this time his knife sliced across the monkey's chest, and red blood stained the gleaming white fur.

"*Chak!*" cried the clip-tailed monkey, with hurt and surprise in his luminous eyes.

The warrior laughed and lunged again. This time the monkey didn't wait for the blow. He somersaulted into an upper branch with a high-pitched shriek, and the Raja's son was thrown off balance, and tumbled forward into a mass of sharp pine needles. Three big black monkeys leaped from a nearby tree, onto the pine branch where the angry warrior was stranded. They moved out along the rough bough with their yellow teeth bared, forcing the Raja's son to scoot backward, to where the limb was too thin to bear his weight. The branch swayed ominously. A tribesman shot a sharp rock from the ground, which struck one of the black monkeys in the snout, and sent him sailing and shrieking to his death on the ground.

The remaining two monkeys continued to advance on the Raja's son, who edged backward . . . He flung his kris at the oncoming monkeys, grasped the branch with his two strong hands, and swung down—into a sturdier bough. The knife missed its mark and sailed to the earth.

"Come and get me!" he called to the monkeys above him with a barking laugh. The monkeys chattered and threw pinecones at his head.

The white monkey, his chest matted with blood, grasped Madai with a spidery arm and hurtled across an abyss to a distant pine tree. Madai had a sensation of falling . . . *falling* . . . and pine needles scratched at his face. The white monkey's leathery free hand clasped at a bough with a sure grip, and hauled them onto a safer perch.

They watched the pair of black monkeys drive the Raja's son down from the tree with a hail of pinecones—while dodging the tribes' lethal stones. When the Raja's son reached the ground, the black pair leaped to join Madai and their white leader.

A sharp rock whizzed near Madai's ears and he ducked his startled head.

The monkeys linked their sinuous arms and formed a living chain to a farther tree—and passed Madai across the chasm. The rest of the monkey troop joined them, chakking with excitement. In a flurry of motion they created monkey chains from tree to tree, downhill through the dense forest, tossing Madai between them like a piece of ripe fruit. Madai's head whirled as strong monkey arms grasped him, and flung him from monkey to monkey and tree to tree, until they were no longer in the upland pines, but down in the lowlands, swinging and chakking and throwing Madai through the branches of a massive desa mango tree. Finally the monkeys let him go, and he climbed shakily down from the mango, to the familiar ground of the orchards near his home.

"Many thanks . . ." called Madai.

"*Chak* . . . *Chak* . . . *Chak!*" The clip-tailed monkey leader shouted his victory against the ape-eating First-Ones, his chest still stained with dried blood. Then jabbering and chakking, the monkey troop sailed away through the trees while Madai trudged wearily home.

Madai's startling story of his capture and escape was repeated all over the island—except at the government police office. The First-Ones had kidnapped him to heal their dying Raja. In the scuffle the Moonbird had been chipped, and the Garuda had flown away. He was unable to help the chief, so the old man died, and Madai escaped alone through the dark forest during the night. That was his story, and Madai wouldn't say anything more—and he knew the awed First-Ones would keep his secrets safely.

"I can't stay here any longer—this place gives me the *creeps* and we're leaving for Bali right away. *Will* you come with us?" demanded Jana, nervously pacing the polished teak deck of the yacht and sipping a bourbon and soda.

"No, ma'am. The Garuda has flown away, so I can no longer help you."

"Flown away? I see . . . What about the *other* one—the witch?"

". . . I think she flew away too. Please *try* to forget about her."

Jana snorted. "Have it your own way. When you cured me I promised you money to repair the island, so here's money. All the cash I brought. There's plenty of money for cement, and plenty of money for you and your girlfriend to join us if terminal boredom changes your mind. Maybe your spirits will fly back one of these days, eh, Madai? Maybe you can still see America and live all your dreams. You'd like that, wouldn't you? Just send me a cable and I'll take care of everything. I'll be waiting to hear from you."

Jana handed Madai a fat envelope filled with more cash than he'd ever seen. Ernie, Sonia, and Paul embraced him with warm farewells. Ernie broke off to finish his pizza and canned asparagus from the yacht's well-stocked galley.

The next morning Madai and Lasmi stood at the dock holding hands, and watching the sleek white yacht sail the foreigners away.

"Are you sorry you didn't go with them?" asked Lasmi, tightening the blue-flowered sash and sarong around her narrow waist.

"A little," admitted Madai.

"Will you change your mind like the foreign woman said?"

"No, I could never do what she asked."

"Because the Garuda is gone? I can't believe that it flew away!"

"It's true." Madai plucked the moonstone image from the silver amulet around his neck. "Remember how shiny the Moonbird used to be? When I was struggling with the First-Ones the beak cracked —and the light poured out. Maybe they frightened the Moonbird." Madai was embarrassed to admit the truth about his breaking the image in anger—even to Lasmi.

"The First-Ones *are* very ugly, with all that matted hair and streaked with mud, and they smell funny too—but I think it's hard to frighten a *god*. Maybe the Garuda will come back soon."

"Maybe." Lasmi always had asked difficult questions, even when they were children playing together in the passion fruit groves. "So what will you do now?"

After a long moment of hesitation, Madai lifted his sensitive hand to stroke the softness of Lasmi's cheek, and the long black hair that cascaded down her back. "I'll do what I always wanted to do—I'll marry you and live like an ordinary man. We'll have bright, sturdy babies to care for us when we're old—if you still want a bald-headed weakling like me."

"Of course I still want you, Madai! I never loved any man but you. But shouldn't we wait to see if the Garuda returns?"

"I've waited long enough . . . I don't want to wait any longer."

Madai visited Lasmi's shabby family compound, on the swampy edge of the desa, on three successive days, carrying mounds of betrothal gifts. He brought colorful batik cloth, sacks of rice, preserved fruit and tinned milk, mosquito repellent coils and matches, and rubber thongs from the Chinese store.

Each day Lasmi's lame mother accepted the gifts with considerable glee. Finally her daughter would wed the strange one who'd kept her waiting all these barren years. At last poor Lasmi would be spared the terrible fate of an unmarried woman—to suckle a giant caterpillar in the afterlife.

On the fourth day, the wedding ceremony took place in Madai's family compound. The carved jackwood altar was decorated for the occasion with fluttering ceremonial banners, palm fronds and flowers woven into towers, and baskets piled high with rice and ripe fruit. The village musicians played their bubbling gamelans, and the rich, curried scents of the wedding feast floated in the moist air. The white-robed priest sat before the altar, under a ceremonial brocade umbrella, intoning the wedding chants. The family and the villagers were dressed in festive brocades.

The men of the desa carried Madai and Lasmi in gilded litters to the altar, and held silk umbrellas over their heads as the music flowed around them. Lasmi was draped in a crimson and gold sarong and a lacy yellow *kebaya* blouse. A tall gilded headdress of filigreed leather sat proudly on her head, and perfumed flowers were twined in her oiled hair. Her arms were ringed with delicate golden bangles, and a happy smile lit her flushed face.

Madai wore a purple and gilt sarong, tunic, and headband, and carried a glittering brass kris with a jeweled hilt. A red hibiscus flower was tucked jauntily behind one ear. He sat tall and proud above the shoulders of the men who bore his litter.

The gamelans sang sweetly as the priest chanted, and gave Madai and Lasmi holy water to drink from an ornately-worked silver ladle. He fed them rice and fruit from the offering baskets, recited the marriage prayers from old palm-leaf texts, and wafted incense smoke from a tiny charcoal brazier toward them with a palm-frond fan. Then he poured holy water onto their heads—and Madai and Lasmi were wed.

The village musicians played lilting dance music, and a celebration began that would last all night. Giggling boys exploded firecrackers and beaming relatives congratulated each other. At last Madai would take his role as a man of the family and the desa. He would take his proper seat in the meeting pavilion to debate the communal needs of the village, and he would carry on the family line so the ancestors could be reborn in human form.

As for the Garuda, well, maybe it would come back later, but they were too busy celebrating to worry about that now. There was music and dancing. There was rice wine and Australian beer. There were banana leaves piled with nutmeg-flavored rice; and fish stewed with ginger; and chicken cooked in coco-milk and hot peppers; and noodles fried with shrimp, egg, and slivers of onion; and vegetables pickled with brown sugar and chilies; and skewers of charcoal-grilled pork with a sweet-and-spicy peanut sauce; and creamy cinnamon-and-coco-cakes. And a swirl of joy for the bride and groom.

That night Madai tasted the sweet yearnings of the senses for the first time, and slept contentedly in Lasmi's soft embrace.

Madai loved to watch Lasmi. He loved it when the filtered light of the rattan sleeping house made reddish glints in her hair as it flowed across their mat. He loved the sinuous motions of her hands, and the expressions on her pert face as she gravely brewed medicinal herbs and helped his mother with the myriad household tasks. They talked and teased and played endlessly, and Madai thought he could be content forever, watching Lasmi, and being excited and soothed by her voice and her touch. She quickly replaced the Moonbird as the center of his life. She was a cozy niche where his weary soul could rest, and she evoked the laughter that had long lain dormant. He watched her, endlessly fascinated, until she playfully slapped at him and told him to stop staring all the time.

Madai rested and read and ate heartily until he grew sturdy again, and even a bit plump. Everyone in the desa noticed that marriage agreed with Madai. He met with the village council to discuss repairing the temple and irrigation channels that were damaged by the earthquake and typhoon. The extended families had repaired their own compounds, but the entire community would work together on these group projects, because sharing is the *adat*, the common law of the desas.

Madai contributed most of Jana's money for construction materials, which they ordered from the Chinese merchants who live near the dock. But he kept some of the money hidden—just in case. The repairs proceeded smoothly, and Madai felt content.

"You're looking fit and your appetite is back to normal," said his father one night as the family sat around a kerosene lamp, eating rice, fish, and vegetables fried in coco-oil. "I expect you'll be giving us grandchildren soon. More mouths to feed. Maybe it's time to go diving for lobsters again, eh, Madai? You'll get too fat and lazy laying around the house. If diving is too rugged, maybe you'll come out on the fishing boats—we don't have such a *bad* time, you know. You were weak and needed to rest, but now you look strong again. A man must feed his family."

"I know, Bapak. I'll come out on the boats with you soon."

That night Madai went to his sleeping mat in a fretful mood, and dreamed of the Moonbird for the first time. He dreamed that the shining Garuda came to him and carried him again. They soared above the treetops and dived under the creamy water, through sinuous tangles of translucent green seaweed, to the endlessly branching rosy coral reef and the rocky sea floor. They spotted a fat, livid lobster waving its eyestalks and fluttering its long, sensitive feelers.

Madai, the hunter, knew that he couldn't just grab at the lobster, or it would scuttle backward with astonishing speed. He tried to circle the beast, but it turned and watched him warily. With swift and skillful motions, Madai distracted the lobster with one hand, and quickly grabbed it from behind with the other. The crustacean flopped helplessly in his tight grip, then sighed with dismay and went limp. Madai and the lobster eyed each other unhappily. *Why must some creatures eat and others be eaten?* Madai wondered, abruptly releasing the lobster, who pinched his big toe with a mischievous giggle, then quickly scuttled away.

When Madai awoke, he realized that he sorely missed flying the Moonbird, and missed his wondrous powers. Would he never hear the sweet rustle of shimmering wings again? But the moonstone image remained dark and dull.

Madai grew increasingly restless. He didn't want to go out in the boats, but he was bored lying listlessly around the house. His mind strayed more and more often to the Moonbird. His thoughts lingered on flying in the prismatic sunlight and battling the germbugs. He grew quiet and preoccupied, and even Lasmi could seldom make him laugh.

The breezy night of the full-moon festival, a number of villagers ate tainted fish and fell ill, fainting and vomiting. One small boy coughed up lots of blood and died. The families of the afflicted poured into Madai's compound, carrying gifts and begging him to *try* to end the epidemic of food poisoning.

"I *can't!* Don't you understand? The Moonbird no longer glows. I don't have the power to help you. Lasmi will brew some herbs."

But herbs were useless, and three more people died. "He could have *tried,*" the villagers grumbled and grieved.

After the epidemic, Madai asked Lasmi to walk with him in the papaya groves behind the village, and he spoke to her intently. "I want to leave the island. It makes me sad to see the sick ones and know I can't help them."

"Where will you go?" cried Lasmi, dismay in her dark eyes.

"*We'll* go," he assured her. "I saved some of the foreign woman's money. She gave me enough to follow her to America, but that's not what I want. We could see Bali, Djakarta—maybe even Australia. We're young enough to learn city skills and get jobs. I want to hide in a vast city—where nobody has ever heard of Madai the *Healer.*"

"It'll be strange and lonely . . ." said Lasmi.

"I know, but we'll see interesting new things—I can no longer live happily on the island. The sick ones and all the memories haunt me."

"Women dress differently in cities—I wonder how I'd look in blue jeans?" asked Lasmi with a tentative smile.

28

Madai and Lasmi began eagerly planning their sojourn to the outside world. They borrowed guidebooks and timetables from Father Hans, and bought knapsacks from the Chinese store. They would explore all the marvels—then they'd decide whether to settle elsewhere or return to the island.

One fine morning, Lasmi went to pick herbs in the mists of the forests. Her mind was full of exotic place names, and she hummed a temple song. She had reached a slender hand to strip fungus from the soft bark of a rotting, fallen tree when she heard a sudden hissing sound. She pulled her hand back, afraid that a viper lurked behind the log. Then something strange popped up from a mound of forest debris, and Lasmi leaped backward with a startled cry. The eerie thing hovered above her head with a flickering blue glow as Lasmi stared in horror.

It was the broken shard of a white face with tangled copper hair, one cold, bulging eye, and a tusked, leering mouth that hissed, "He thinks he can escape so easily . . ."

Lasmi shrieked and ran down the pathway, but the face bobbed above her like a malevolent balloon.

"*Escape* . . ." echoed an iridescent blue dragonfly.

But Lasmi couldn't escape. "Who *are* you?" she cried.

"I *see* Lasmi . . ." sneered the shattered face.

Lasmi raced along the narrow pathways of the dense forest, but she couldn't elude the monster that hovered over her head. She reached an algae-covered pond and dived skillfully among the reeds, beneath the still green water.

"*Escape* . . ." buzzed the blue dragonfly, circling the pond.

The ghastly face slid beneath the scummy water, bubbling . . . "I *see* Lasmi . . ."

She jumped out of the pond, streaming wet, her long black hair flecked with bright green algae. She ran from the apparition and crouched in the narrow hollow of an embracing ironwood tree, but the gruesome face swooped down at her like a bat. "I *see* Lasmi . . ."

There was no place to run or hide. She tried to scream, but her throat was frozen with panic. Lasmi scampered back toward the desa, to the village temple, where the priests could help her. But when she reached the crumbling sandstone gateway, draped with pink flowering bougainvillea, the terrible creature blocked her way so that she couldn't enter the temple grounds. The face darted at her, laughing, and chased her away from the temple. Lasmi began to cry as she ran.

She raced between the fields to her mother's compound, stumbling and sobbing, with the monster hovering just above her head, pulsing and hissing in her ear . . . "I *see* Lasmi . . ." She reached her mother's shabby wicker gate and almost slipped inside, but the witch swooped at her with tusks bared, and wouldn't let her pass.

"*Why* are you chasing me?" wept Lasmi as she ran toward Madai's compound. "Leave me alone!"

Now the throbbing specter was everywhere, swirling and enveloping her until she could only see the sneering shard of Rangda, with her cold eye and wicked fangs and matted copper hair, whirling and hissing all around her. Until Lasmi gave one final cry, and collapsed in the mud near Madai's gate.

Some village women found her like that and carried her home. Madai's mother fanned her unconscious daughter-in-law with a knowing smile. "I once fainted like that when I was pregnant with poor Dawan." The village women nodded with comfortable sighs.

Madai bounded down from the sleeping house, where he'd been reading a book on Australia. His face looked grim. "Wake up, Lasmi! What's wrong?"

Madai and his mother examined her, but they could find no injury. She breathed normally, and there were no marks or bruises—except the curious scum of drying algae in her hair.

They washed her face with cold water, and gradually Lasmi awoke, whimpering and thrashing her arms as if trying to push something away. She opened her eyes, sat up abruptly, and burst into tears.

"What's wrong . . . What happened?"

"Something horrible was chasing after me!"

"You mean an animal in the forest? Lucky it didn't bite you," said his mother.

"Not an animal, Ibu. A leyak-spirit! It was white and ugly and hairy, with pointed teeth. It jumped all around me and made a terrible hissing sound."

"Maybe it was an insect or a bat," said Ibu.

"It was no insect or bat," insisted Lasmi. "It was everywhere at once, *chasing* me. I ran through the forest and jumped into the pond, but it followed me. I tried to hide in the temple and at my mother's house, but it leaped at me and wouldn't let me inside. I wanted to call for help and to run home, but it was everywhere—like a nightmare! It looked like a mask from the temple . . . like the broken face of Rangda. It flew all around me and hissed . . . 'I *see* Lasmi.'"

Madai's face tightened with anger, and a coco-shell filled with cool water slipped from his hand.

"People see strange things in the forest," soothed Ibu. "Maybe it was a big owl darting for lizards. Maybe you felt strange from the sun; that happens sometimes. Nothing bit you, so you'll be all right. You might be with child, which made you feel faint. You must rest and care for yourself. Your travels can wait a while. Our first grandchild must be healthy and strong."

Madai led Lasmi to the sleeping house. "It wasn't a bird or animal," she insisted. "And I know I'm not with child—my menses just ended. It was something terrible. A leyak-spirit—but why did it chase *me?*"

"Maybe it was using you to attack me," said Madai gloomily.

"Why did it come now? I'm frightened. Hold me tightly, Madai."

He drew his tawny arms around her shivering body. "You're shaking with a cold fever," he said.

Then he noticed a coarse, coppery hair tangled among the soft dark waves that flowed down Lasmi's back. He held it up to the filtered light, where it glowed like a dull copper wire. They both stared at the hair with disgust.

"Is this yours?" asked Madai.

"Of course not!" Lasmi whimpered and covered her face with her hands. "My hair doesn't look like that. It belongs to the leyak—don't *touch* it!"

Madai stared at the hair as the rage grew inside him. "Damn you, Rangda, you're back!" he muttered. "What do you want with us? Why can't you leave us alone? You follow me like a plague follows the sick ones. No matter what I do you pursue me, like a tumor that invades one part of the body, then another—and then you're everywhere! Whenever I think you're finally gone, you still lurk and wait to destroy me. I've cured so many unfortunates—why can't I heal myself of Rangda? Is there some medicine or healer whose touch or prayers can make you go away? Or will you always be there, malignantly hiding and waiting to trap me, until I'm finally too weak to fight back? Get away, Rangda! Leave us alone. Find someone else to play your ugly games."

The next day Lasmi complained of feeling dizzy and weak. She looked pale. This was understandable, since she'd had quite a shock, and hadn't slept well that night. Madai's mother urged her to rest, and nodded to Bapak with a knowing smile.

A week passed and she felt no better. The dizzy weakness lingered, and she could hardly lift her head from the mat or hold any solid food. She complained that her head and limbs ached. Her skin looked dull and sallow as wax. Even matronly Ibu began to worry.

The nursing nun at the mission drew a sample of Lasmi's blood, and Madai paid the amiable captain of the mail boat to carry it in his ice chest to the hospital on Bali. They waited tensely for the report. The following week the captain returned with an inconclusive message.

The tests showed that her white blood count was very high, which could be an unusual infection—or even leukemia. If she still felt ill next week, she could come to the hospital for an examination.

Madai knew that no hospitals and no examinations would help her. Lasmi grew steadily weaker, and Madai could feel her vitality seeping away, until she seemed almost transparent.

Madai couldn't wait. If he wanted to save Lasmi, he had to find the Moonbird.

V

Madai searched for the Moonbird . . .

29

But *where* would he find the precious and elusive Moonbird?

Lasmi grew weaker every day, and Madai was like a powerless old man, unable to help her. He was furious. He couldn't let her die . . . He *couldn't*. There must be some way to save her. He would do *anything* . . . anything. Resolutely he marched to the ancient village temple.

"*Rangda!*" he called. "Where are you, Rangda? I must talk to you."

There was a flicker and a hiss in a red-flowered hibiscus shrub, and the phosphorescent shard of the witch's face hovered among the delicately cupped blossoms.

"I've changed my mind," said Madai.

"*So . . . ?*" smiled the shard of the witch.

"So I'll do what you and Jana wish," said Madai. "I'll become your servant and help augment your foul powers, and kill at the foreign woman's command—if you'll heal Lasmi now."

"Should I trust you to keep such promises?" hissed Rangda.

"You can trust me—Lasmi is your hostage. If I don't obey, you can always attack her again."

"Perhaps that's so," admitted Rangda, her solitary cold eye widening with interest. "What makes you suppose I can save Lasmi?"

"Don't play word games with me, witch. You made her ill. You *must* be able to help her—then I'll become your servant."

"Perhaps you're *already* my servant," sneered Rangda. "Why say I sickened her? I merely saw her . . . *saw.*"

"Stop it!" shouted Madai, smashing his fist into the shrub, snapping twigs and scattering veined leaves and scarlet flower petals, which floated slowly to the ground. Madai lifted his hand and saw that a jagged twig had cut a bloody gash on his palm. "I'm tired of hearing that, year after year. You *know* your evil eye sends misfortune—we *both* know it! Why do you lie to me again and again? I've agreed to do any evil thing you ask—if you'll heal her."

"Perhaps," smiled Rangda, hovering just above Madai's head in the misty sunlight. "You must wash your hand, my son. I see fresh blood . . ."

Madai returned to the compound and bent anxiously over Lasmi's sleeping mat. He spooned coco-water between her parched, cracked lips, bathed her wasted face, and tenderly massaged her pulses, but she grew no stronger.

"Copper hair," murmured Lasmi, twisting feverishly on her mat.

That night Madai returned to the dark stillness of the temple. The thatched pagodas looked spectral in the soft sliver of moonlight.

"Why isn't she stronger?" Madai demanded of Rangda. "When the Moonbird heals the sick ones, they grow better right away."

"So ask that sparrow god to save her," sneered Rangda from her wicker hut on the altar.

Days passed, and there was still no improvement in Lasmi's health. Madai realized that Rangda was lying to him. The Antagonist *didn't* have the power to undo her own curses, no matter what terrible promises he made.

"You *haven't* healed her," accused Madai one dank, drizzly dawn. "Your presence only frightens her."

"I never said I had powers to save," said Rangda sullenly.

"Try, damn you, *try!*"

"Rangda tries and *tries*, my son," pouted the shard, darting like a firefly between the crumbling, overgrown temple gateways.

"I'm *not* your son! You have no power to heal—only to curse and cause pain. Leave us alone, filthy one. Don't come near us again!" Madai picked up a sharp rock and hurled it at the witch, but she laughed and bobbed away.

Then she swooped down so her shattered face, with the white tusked cheek and tangled copper hair, was just at Madai's eye level. "Rangda tries and *tries*, but you aren't satisfied. There's nothing more to show you, my son." Rangda stared at him with a malicious scowl—then closed her single eye.

"Are you sleeping, witch?" asked Madai with grim surprise. "Why have you closed your eye?"

"Why should Rangda assist your stupid schemes?" hissed the Antagonist, her eye still tightly shut. "You send me away, then summon me to toss rocks and insults. Rangda doesn't wish to see for you. See for yourself if you can . . . *See* . . ." Then the flickering shard of Rangda disappeared.

Now even Rangda was angry and had abandoned him. Now he

had no powers left at all. No awful gift that he could barter for Lasmi's life. Even offering himself as servant of the witch couldn't save her, and Lasmi would perish soon—unless he could summon the Moonbird.

Lasmi grew weaker. She floated in and out of delirious dreams as her vitality ebbed. Madai was desperate. He thought of nothing except finding the Moonbird. He ached for the sound of rustling wings, the sight of gleaming feathers, the tensing of proud muscles as they rose into the air and entered the body—Lasmi's body, where Madai would slash and fight until every abnormal cell was destroyed.

He sat in the banyan grove day after day, fasting and calling to the Moonbird until he grew parched and hoarse. No Garuda appeared. Soon the strange wasting illness would be too far advanced, and Lasmi would be too far away for even a god to save her. Her skin felt like faded rose petals, and sometimes she hardly knew he was there beside her. How could he helplessly watch her die? The gods grow opium poppies to ease pain—but *nothing* could ease Madai's mind.

Madai wept in his sleeping mat for himself and Lasmi when he realized his quest might not succeed.

At dawn he rose to the lusty crowing of roosters, tucked a faded sarong around his waist, slipped a few things into a carrying pouch, and filled a bottle with clean water. He slipped on rubber thong sandals and hurried out of the wicker compound, and away from the village before anyone could waken and delay him. He would wander the wild forests and hills of the island, searching for the Moonbird.

He stopped first at the old temple at the edge of the desa. The three thatched pagodas sat silently in the humid gray dawn. Madai entered the seven-tiered central temple. The shattered mask of Rangda had been repaired, but the jagged lines of breakage were still clearly visible. Rotund green flies buzzed sullenly around the fruit offerings before the witch, but she remained stubbornly silent.

He knelt at the altar of Visnu the Preserver. The elaborately painted crimson and white image of the god, with its golden headdress, rode on the back of an ornate wooden Garuda, painted white and pale green, which stood with outstretched wings upon the backs of golden, intertwining Naga-dragons.

Madai prayed fervently to Lord Visnu and his impassive servants, then he slipped out of the sandstone temple gates. He left the desa pathways behind as he entered the dense green jungles, where he wandered aimlessly, pausing in secluded groves to call the chipped, faded Moonbird—who wouldn't answer.

He soon found his way to the network of paths and paddies of a neighboring desa, for the ancient forest was giving way to expanding clearings, for farms to feed the growing population of hungry islanders. A band of women worked the paddies, with muddy sarongs tucked loosely around their waists. They chanted work songs, laughed and gossiped, and carried placid, large-eyed infants on their hips. The women recognized Madai and approached him. A young matron showed him a painful boil on her neck. Another complained that her baby had an earache, and an older woman with shriveled skin whispered that her vision was blurred and she feared cataracts and blindness. They'd heard that he sought to restore his powers to heal his wife—and they hoped he'd remember them too.

Madai promised not to forget them, but explained they must leave him alone. They followed him for a while, at a respectful distance, and others joined their ragged band. Finally he gestured at them angrily to go away. He needed solitude and silence to find the Moonbird, but where could he find seclusion on this crowded island?

The sun grew hot, and the air was heavy and wet after the monsoons. The palm fronds drooped and aimless mosquitoes and flies were drawn to the scent of his sweat. He brushed them away in annoyance. He ate nothing all that day, and drank only small sips of water. He pushed deeply into the bush, not stopping to rest, and trying to avoid village fields and orchards.

By dusk he'd eluded his followers. He found a row of austere, towering trees that led to the ruins of an abandoned temple of black lava rock, overgrown with thorny brush and purple flowering weeds. He made his camp on the rubble of the altar, and dozed fitfully and called to the Moonbird.

The only answer was a subaudible rumble from the massive roots of the stately row of broad-leaved trees that twined beneath the earth where Madai slept. The tree roots whispered to him all through the night of strength and tenacity, but their slow, droning words were difficult to comprehend.

The next day he set out on his wanderings again, and came upon a familiar-looking pond in a pretty forest glade. Frilly ferns and bright pink lotuses grew at the edge of the water. With a shock, he realized that he'd circled back, and this pond had been a favorite bathing spot for Lasmi, Dawan, and the other girls of the desa. He gazed tearfully at the still pool, sad memories of their laughter and gossipy chatter churning inside him. He idly pulled at a bit of dried moss that clung to a gnarled tree.

"Stop that!" cried a soft, oddly familiar voice.

"*Dawan?*"

"Why did you waken me?"

"It's Madai. What are you doing here?"

"I'm *dead*. You mustn't disturb me."

"I didn't know you were here," said Madai, tears burning his eyes. "How does it feel—to be dead?"

"It doesn't feel like anything. At first I was terribly sad and lonely —and angry. All the villagers wandered in and out of our compound, laughing and talking and eating while the priests wrapped me in a cold shroud. I tried to get their attention by dropping things and startling them—but it didn't work. Nobody noticed me at all. Then I wandered for a timeless time in a strange and beautiful garden. I was all alone—and I couldn't leave. I waited for the cremation fires to send my spirit to the far shore to join the ancestors. I waited until everything slowly faded away and I grew very sleepy. So I curled up inside that bed of dried moss beside my favorite pond. Then there was nothing until you woke me. Don't be in such a hurry to know what it's like. You'll find out soon enough—the only mystery is when and where and how."

"I've missed you, Dawan. So much has happened, and I needed to talk to you. The Moonbird has left me—and Lasmi is very ill."

"You must climb *up*, Madai."

Then a sudden gust of wind blew the tuft of dry moss into the humid air. "Climb up, Madai . . ." she repeated. Then her voice was still.

"Climb up . . . Climb *up* . . ." sang the pastel water lilies that ringed the pond.

"Dawan!" cried Madai. But the bit of dry moss sailed away in the breeze. He camped beside the pool, hoping she might return, but she was gone—back to her lonely garden.

The next morning he continued his wanderings, heading inland toward the hills. In the afternoon of his third day without solid food or sound sleep, he reached the foothills of the volcanic mountains in the center of the island, and began to climb the isolated slopes. He felt dizzy from lack of food and rest, but as he climbed higher, and finally reached the windy forests of mountain pines, he felt cooler and somehow refreshed. Nobody lived this high and Madai was finally alone. He gazed at the chipped, clouded image and called loudly to the Moonbird, but still there was no answer.

He continued to climb. He found a tangle of sweet, tiny wild berries and ate his fill. He filled his water bottle from a bubbling spring and lay like a lizard on a flat, warm rock. As the half-moon rose, he fell into a deep, dreamless sleep. The moon was high in the sky when he was suddenly wakened by a pulsing chant . . .

". . . *Chak* . . . *Chak* . . . *Chak!*"

Madai leaped up from his rock, and in the light of the half-moon he saw the monkey troop tumbling through the trees, somersaulting from branch to branch. Their white, clip-tailed leader paused, suspended from a thick vine, and stared down at Madai with surprised jet eyes.

"*Hanuman!*" called Madai. "I'm searching for the Moonbird—have you seen it?"

"*Chak . . . Chak . . .* I wish I had! I'm gathering an army of allies to battle the crow-demons, who are eating all the fruit of the life-giving tree on the mountain in the center of the universe. Will you join us, healer-man—though I must warn you of difficulty and danger."

Madai thought about it. He owed a debt of honor and gratitude to the powerful ape-chief who rescued him from the First-Ones, and his search for the Moonbird was going nowhere. Perhaps he should join the monkey army and travel *up* to the mountain in the center of the universe, where he might find the Garuda's secluded nesting cavern, or meet some other magical being who could help him. Just as Rama, in the *Ramayana*, had joined forces with Hanuman to rescue Sita. And what did he care about difficulty and danger when Lasmi was so close to death?

"I'm your ally and I'll join you," Madai called to Hanuman. "If you think a weakling like me can aid your battle—but if we meet the Garuda, I must return to the island at once."

"You are slight, but your mind is quick—who knows how you might help us, and perhaps I can further your quest. Climb on my shoulders." The clip-tailed monkey general swooped down on his vine and plucked Madai from the rock. He scrambled onto the ape's broad back and found a comfortable spot, clinging to the warm, thick white fur of Hanuman's strong neck. The monkey troop continued on their way, whooping and chakking, swinging through the twining branches of the trees, seeking allies.

A great swarm of iridescent blue dragonflies joined them, flying in a V-formation behind their humming queen.

The army of forest creatures reached the shore of the island, and paused on a narrow beach ringed with fluttering coco-palms. The frothy ocean looked like purple jade in the moonlight. Madai wondered where they would go, for monkeys have no power to fly to other realms.

Then the white monkey made a running leap and vaulted into a giant somersault. It was all Madai could do to cling to the coarse hair of his neck as they whizzed through the air. They hurtled across the water—a vast distance, and landed in a desolate range of gleaming iron mountains, where the air was thin and nothing grew in the rusty dust.

"*Beh!*" exclaimed Madai.

"Hold tight," rumbled the monkey-general—who seemed to be growing larger. Another leaping somersault, and they landed on the slopes of glowing copper mountains as the monkey grew even bigger.

Another leap across endless black waters, and they stood among silver mountains that shone with their own light, for there was no longer any moon or stars in the airless black overhead. The clip-tailed monkey was now much taller and broader than any man. Another hurtling somersault, and they landed among bright golden mountains that glimmered like morning sunlight.

The great monkey bellowed a great whoop and made another great leap, and landed on the slopes of a mountain so high that its peak could never be seen. The jagged boulders on the hillsides were made of precious stones—turquoise and jade, amethyst, ruby and lapis lazuli—that flashed in the crystalline light of a very young sun. They had reached the mountain in the center of the universe, and the troop of chakking monkeys and the formation of droning dragonflies followed them closely. Madai clung to the great monkey's white-furred neck, and gazed around him in wonder.

From the center of the mountain there sprouts an immense tree, whose top can't be seen because it rises from the obscure peak. Its leafy branches hang at all levels of the mountain, laden with fragrant white flowers and a creamy white fruit that splits open when it ripens, to drip a rich, milky, honey-sweet nectar. The gods and demigods who dwell on the slopes take their nourishment from that fruit.

"Look!" growled Hanuman.

A flock of huge black crows flew screeching above them, then dived down and tore ravenously at the fruit with their sinuous beaks. Madai stared in terror at the crows, for these weren't the greedy, thieving birds of the island. Their feathers were made of satiny black obsidian—sharp as razors. Their beaks were shaped like wavy kris dagger blades, and their talons were tipped with viper venom.

"The gods and demigods who live on the mountain will perish if they can't sip the nectar, but the fierce crow-demons won't let them near it. They swarm onto the mountain from the demons' realm, and attack any deity who tries to touch the ripe fruit. The gods are growing weak, and when they die the demons will control the mountain in the center of the universe. I was called from my retreat on your island to help the gods battle the evil crows," explained Hanuman.

As they watched, a small female demigod crept behind boulders of lapis and jade to the thick branches of the tree. She had bulging round eyes and delicately pointed tusks, and a mat of soft white scales—and she was pretty in her own, demigoddess way. She hid behind a rock and tried to grasp a ripe, creamy fruit with her small, scaley claw. The crows wheeling overhead spotted her with their beady red eyes and screamed in a mocking tone as they darted down and swiped the fruit from her grasp. They slashed at her with knife-edged talons and beaks. The demigoddess whimpered and tried to scamper away, but the flock of screaming crows swarmed after her, cutting and stabbing until her scales were wet with colorless blood.

"They'll kill *Drolma!*" bellowed Hanuman, bounding forward so his massive white body stood between the little demigoddess and the crows. The chakking monkey troop and droning dragonfly formation surged forward and confronted the crows, who shrieked their rage. The demigoddess scrambled onto the white monkey's back beside Madai, and licked at her wounds. The crows swooped down and slashed at the monkeys, drawing earth-red blood.

"*Chak . . . Chak . . . Chak!*" chattered the monkeys, picking up rocks of bright blue turquoise and hurtling them with deadly aim at the crows, who fell from the sky screeching, and crumbled on the jeweled slopes in heaps of broken obsidian feathers and rusty blood.

For each crow that fell, a hundred more soared through the crystal air to join the evil flock, attracted by the sounds of battle and the scent of blood, until the bright blue sky was layered with circling, screaming crows, their razor feathers glinting in the sunlight.

"*Beh!*" cried Madai. "There's no end to them—like the germbugs, but they attack with minds that are ferociously cunning."

A crow dipped down and whipped its beak across Madai's neck, drawing a line of bright red droplets. He reached up his hand to push the nasty bird away, and sliced his fingers on the razor feathers. A squadron of dragonflies came to his aid, fluttering and humming around the crow to distract it.

What would the Moonbird do now? Madai wondered. The Garuda would ask a dry, laconic riddle such as: "How does your mother chase crows from the rice paddies?—with a *scarecrow!*" But how could they make a scarecrow on the mountain in the center of the universe?

The battle increased in frenzy. The sun was obscured by the wheeling flock of screaming obsidian crows, who lashed at the chakking monkeys. Some of the ape warriors had fallen in puddles of fur and sticky simian blood. The remaining monkeys grimly hurled their lethal turquoise missiles at the crows, who tumbled from the sky. But still there were more—and more. The dragonflies buzzed at the crows, darting in erratic patterns to startle and confuse the malevolent birds.

Then Madai had an idea. The glistening blue dragonflies were skilled at flying in formation. If they formed themselves into the shape of a vast Garuda, they could fly toward the crows and frighten them—like a scarecrow!

Madai climbed onto the heaving shoulder of the battling monkey-general, tugged at his ear to get his attention, and whispered his plan. Hanuman nodded with a quizzical smile and summoned the dragonfly Queen to communicate the plot.

She buzzed her assent and led her troops away from the battle, behind an outcropping of immense amethyst boulders. The swarming crows hardly noticed the departure of the pesky flies as they swooped and lashed at the bleeding monkey troop.

From behind the amethyst boulders, there rose with stately grace a gleaming blue Garuda, whose wingspan was so wide it filled half the sky. The blue Garuda slowly approached the circling flock of crows with a menacing drone, and the crows squalled with surprise. They darted and slashed at the Garuda, but there was no way they could wound its flesh, which was made of some ethereal blue substance that drifted away—then rejoined the body again.

The crows shrieked with terror and began to retreat—for all beings know that a magical Garuda has more power than mere crows.

The giant eagle-god calmly herded the crows down the slope of the mightiest mountain, away from the branches of the life-giving tree. The monkey troop followed behind, chakking and aiming a volley of deadly turquoise pellets.

From their hiding places in clefts along the jeweled slopes, the gods and demigods emerged, gnashing their ivory tusks and waving their golden krises. Madai proudly rode the back of the clip-tailed monkey-general, and looked behind him in awe. Here were all the carved images of the temple come to life: humanoid or animal, half human and demi-animal, neither human nor animal, forms that were startlingly beautiful and wildly grotesque.

The deities formed a well-armed ring to guard their precious tree —for the vicious crows had originally taken them by surprise. Now they'd be prepared to defend their life source with well-honed weapons that were a match for any crow.

The dragonflies, in the form of an enormous Garuda, drove the wailing black crows away from the mountain in the center of the universe, beyond the realm of gold and silver peaks, to the land of barren copper mountains. The exhausted crow-demons fell from the sky to the glowing copper hills, and watched with angry red eyes as the majestic Garuda sailed away. When it was finally out of sight of the crows, it separated into myriad iridescent blue dragonflies, led by a Queen who floated back to the central mountain, humming with glee.

"You're a warrior, healer-man," said the monkey-general. "Your mind remained impeccably calm in battle, yet you're a man of compassion. If you were a monkey, I'd invite you to join our troop."

"That's high praise and I thank you, Hanuman. If I were a monkey, I'd gladly join your troop," said Madai.

The white-scaled demigoddess leaped off Hanuman's back and capered into the branches of the tree, where she stuffed her tusked mouth with fruit, making glad cooing sounds and happily licking the nectar from her delicately scaled claws. Then with a mischievous little laugh, she tossed ripe, creamy fruit at Hanuman and Madai.

The white ape leaped and caught the flying fruit, and ate it with a deep rumble of laughter. Madai reached up and plucked a succulent white globe from the clear air and popped it in his mouth. The taste was indescribably sweet and delicious, and the nectar filled him with strength and vitality.

Perhaps these will restore Lasmi, thought Madai, catching more fruit, which he tucked in his carrying pouch.

"The fruit isn't for mortals," warned Hanuman. "You can't take it back with you."

"But *I* ate it—and I'm a mortal," said Madai.

"Perhaps," said the clip-tailed monkey, with an enigmatic smile. "If you can eat the fruit, perhaps you *are* ready to join us."

"No. I must go back now—to the island. Lasmi is waiting."

"The dragonflies will carry you," said Hanuman. "I'll stay here, on the mountain in the center of the universe. I've been away too long, fighting too many battles in the realm of troubles, where new conflicts always wait to catch my monkey mind. I'll rest here a while, and romp and play with the demigoddess, Drolma, in the branches of the life-giving tree."

"You've become my friend and I'll miss you," said Madai.

"Perhaps we'll join forces again someday—and remember to climb *up,* Madai," said Hanuman.

The gleaming blue dragonflies formed a ring and lifted him into the clear air. The little demigoddess tossed him a final globe of fruit —then threw one at Hanuman that hit his white-furred brow with a sticky splash. The large-eyed demigoddess shrieked with laughter and raced away into the branches of the tree. Hanuman followed after her, tumbling mirthfully and somersaulting through the boughs until they were too high for Madai to see. The monkey troop raced behind them, cavorting and whooping and chakking.

The ring of humming blue dragonflies sailed across the black waters, past the gold and silver mountains, beyond the copper and iron hills where the hungry crow-demons sullenly picked at the barren soil; until they reached the volcanic slopes of Mount Alāka on their home island. The glistening dragonflies dropped Madai gently to the earth, then drifted away, still humming.

Madai had returned to the land of conflicts. He looked anxiously in his carrying pouch for the life-giving fruit, which he hoped would restore Lasmi. As Hanuman had warned, he found nothing but dust, for only immortals can eat the fruit of the mighty tree in the center of the universe.

He knew he must climb *up* the steep slopes of the massive volcano, and continue his search for the Moonbird.

31

The steep flanks of the volcano had no pathways, and the sharp black lava gravel slashed Madai's exposed feet until they were raw. No wondrous beings appeared to whisk him through the air—only his sore, bleeding feet trudging upward.

Soon he passed the stunted forests of the tree line. The air was thin and crisp, and a whining breeze sent wisps of cottony fog across the lapis blue sky. At this altitude there grew only mosses and rare wild orchids, sparse mountain grasses and low, scrubby wildflowers that hugged the porous volcanic rocks.

As he climbed, the breeze brought the scent of sulphur fumes. The ground cover grew increasingly scant, and a chill wind bit at his bare skin. The water in his bottle was almost gone, and he rationed himself to tiny sips that left Madai thirsting for more. The thin air made his mind feel vague.

He heard a sound of gurgling water ahead. But when he reached the spot, he found a foul, jagged sinkhole of bubbling gray mud emitting poisonous odors, ringed by long green streamers of slimy, heat-loving lichen. He trudged upward . . .

Finally he reached the rim of the volcanic crater. A great expanse of desolate black lava tumbled as far as Madai could see, punctuated by the hissing white plumes of steam vents and the gurgling vapors of hot mud pots. Madai stood at the rim of the volcano and shouted to the Moonbird, but the only answer was the keening wind.

Then he saw a very strange sight. Perched directly on the warm bed of jagged lava rocks was a tiny thatch hut. Outside the hut sat a naked, sinewy old man with long, thin white hair, hollow cheeks, and a wispy beard that covered much of his frail, withered body. The old man had a plump fish stuck onto the end of a sharpened stick, and he was cooking the fish slowly over a steamy spring of bubbling, boiling water.

Madai was tremendously annoyed. He'd climbed Mount Alāka for solitude. He was in no mood to meet a crazed old hermit. The old man spotted Madai with his glittering black eyes, grinned toothlessly, and beckoned to him. Madai walked over to ask if the elder had any water, and saw with surprise that the old man's bare skin was seated directly upon the sharp lava.

"Have some steamed fish?" greeted the graybeard in a high, thin voice. "It's very fresh. I caught it this afternoon."

"Is there a creek nearby then?" asked Madai. "I need some water."

"Oh no," said the elder. "This is an ocean fish."

Madai decided the old man was senile, as he'd suspected. They were days away from the ocean. "Do you have any water?" he asked.

"Here's fresh coco-water," said the old man, offering a large earthen jug.

Madai drank deeply from the jug and felt refreshed by the cool sweetness. "How do you get coconuts up here, Bapak?" he asked.

"I run down and pick them."

"You *do?* That climb is pretty steep, even for a young man like me."

The old man shrugged and tested his fish with a stick to see if it was ready. He was *quite* demented. Probably a grandson came up sometimes to bring him provisions.

"May I fill my bottle from your jug?" asked Madai. "I should be getting on."

"Certainly," smiled the old man. "But where are you going? There's nothing at all beyond here."

"I know. I climbed up for solitude."

"But the sun is setting and it will be dark soon. You might stumble on jagged lava rocks or slip into one of the bottomless vents. There's a cold wind blowing and the sky looks like rain. Why not keep an old grandpa company for tonight?"

He was right. The sky was darkening and deep clouds had formed, pierced by thin flicks of distant lightning. The wind sang mournfully in Madai's ears and made them ache. It would be dangerous out on the lava beds at night. Better to stay in the little hut until morning.

Lightning and thunder cracked through the sky and small hailstones pounded Madai's face and shoulders. He scampered into the hut, but the old man stayed outside, naked in the stormy dusk, patiently steaming his silvery fish over bright, bubbling water.

Then Madai realized he was some kind of leyak-spirit—but was he kind or cruel, and could he help Madai find the Moonbird? The hailstorm passed quickly, and the old man munched his steamed fish in the purple dusk. Madai left the hut and stood beside him.

"Have some fish," he urged.

"I'm not hungry, Bapak," said Madai hesitantly. "I wondered if you could help me find somebody."

"Nobody here but *me!*" cackled the elder.

"I'm looking for a bird—a Garuda."

"I've met the Garuda," smiled the old man, his bright black eyes far away.

"You *have?*" Madai felt a surge of excitement.

"Long ago I dwelt in the Land of Snows with a glowing woman named . . . I no longer remember her name. We were building the great temple of Dza when I was called away. A terrible epidemic of leprosy swept through the river valley of Mother Ganga. It was caused by Basudara, the greedy Naga King, who was blowing the sickness onto the wind."

"Basudara is the Naga King who died recently . . ." said Madai in wonder.

"That's right. Such a splendid funeral procession . . . too bad the rebels spoiled the show by attacking Mahanagini. I see you are familiar with the nether realms. But you must remember that Nagas are *very* long-lived, and this happened very long ago. Basudara was hungry for power in those days, and threatened to blow the leprous winds to every creature in the world. I was summoned to help the inhabitants of the Ganga Valley—for I was called Lotus Born, and I was much stronger in those days. I was sorry to leave that glowing woman . . . what *was* her name? But I couldn't ignore the pleas of the suffering people."

"Such pleas are difficult to ignore," replied Madai with a nod.

"I felt strong enough to swallow the ocean, but I needed an ally. I called upon the great Garuda, who agreed to fly me beneath the sea to the Naga realm. Basudara feared us, and on the spires of his magnificent gilded palace, inlaid with coral and pearls, he stationed fierce silver-scaled guardian dragons whose fiery breath was sharp as swords. We flew right through the dragons' foul breath and landed on the highest tower of the palace. The Naga King and his troops were so frightened that they trembled—causing tidal waves throughout the earth. Thus we conquered them through fear, rather than violence." The old man sliced his fish with the sharp stick.

"Basudara was still reluctant to surrender. 'Who are you?' he bellowed. The Garuda replied, 'I am the eagle-god, here to drink Naga blood and eat dragon flesh.' Basudara was so angry that he swelled to 999 times his ordinary size, grew 999 heads, and devoured the

Garuda—who ate the Naga King's heart and the entrails inside his belly. Then Basudara grew very weak. The Garuda flew out of his mouth, grabbed the main head, and dragged him three times around the mountain in the center of the universe, which caused terrible earthquakes everywhere. Finally Basudara said, 'If you'll spare me, I'll protect and serve you.' So the Garuda and the Nagas became allies. The eagle-god coughed up the Naga King's entrails, which were used to cure the windborne leprosy. Thus the people of the Land of Snows and all the neighboring regions call upon the Garuda for healing. Is that why you're searching in this desolate place?"

"Yes, Bapak! The Garuda I'm seeking looks something like this." Madai lifted the faded moonstone image from the amulet around his neck, and showed it to the strange old man in the light of the rising moon.

"Pretty thing," nodded the elder. "But why is it so cloudy—and why is the beak *chipped?*"

"The beak chipped when I—dropped it against a rock," lied Madai.

"Pity. You should take better care of such a valuable old carving. Here. Give it to me and I'll polish it." The old man snatched the Moonbird from Madai's hand.

"Be careful!"

"I will. Don't fret so impatiently—that's one of your problems, you know."

"What do *you* know of my problems?"

"The wind tells me . . . The wind tells me . . ." hummed the old man, busily polishing the stone image with his long, silky white beard. He blew on it gently. "There, that looks better, doesn't it?" He held the Moonbird up high, so it gleamed brightly in the reflected moonlight.

"It's *shining* again!" Madai's eyes brightened with joy.

"I'll bet you never tried polishing it," accused the elder.

"That's true," laughed Madai.

"Maybe that'll help you," said the old man, yawning deeply. "I must be going now."

Quite abruptly he disappeared, and so did the bubbling hot spring. All that remained was the little hut and the half-eaten fish.

"Bapak, where are you? What's your name?" called Madai. But there was no sound except the crooning wind. Madai sat in the doorway of the hut and held the glistening image up to the reflected moonglow.

"Moonbird," he said softly. "I know you're nearby now. Come *quickly*, please."

32

Without warning came the rustle of wings, and Madai saw the prismatic Moonbird circle overhead. "I'm down here," he called.

The Moonbird landed with a soft thud, and Madai hugged the smooth, cool neck. Then he saw that part of the Garuda's beak was chipped off.

"What happened to your beak?" asked Madai guiltily.

"You cracked it against a rock," snapped the Moonbird.

"I'm so sorry."

"Sorry doesn't renew beaks," observed the Moonbird dryly.

"I needed you so . . . Lasmi is dying; will you help me?"

"Perhaps—*if* I can carry you."

"Who was that old man? Was it your master, Visnu the Preserver?" asked Madai.

"What old man?"

"The one who polished the moonstone, and sat near this hut, eating the cooked fish."

"What hut—what fish?"

Madai realized that the hut and the remains of the fish had also vanished.

"You're tired and your mind is fuzzy. Perhaps it was a figment of your imagination," said the Moonbird.

"But that's what the doctors and scientists say about *you!*"

"Then ask the doctors and scientists to heal Lasmi."

"I'm so happy to see you again," laughed Madai, leaping lightly upon the Garuda's gleaming back. "We must hurry to the desa and Lasmi!"

The Moonbird lifted up abruptly, with a flap of shining wings, and hovered over the desolate, windswept lava beds. There Madai saw something very strange. He'd heard it described many times, and even seen the foreigners' photos, but he'd never before witnessed it with his eyes.

He saw his own body sitting frail and bald at the rim of the volcano, with the steaming, jumbled black lava landscape stretching in every direction. Madai's eyes widened as he watched himself seated with eyelids half closed, a faded sarong tucked around his lean waist, swaying and mumbling in a healing trance.

"That's *me!*" he cried to the Moonbird, both awed and disturbed. "Why have I never seen this before?"

"Yes, that's your physical body," said the Moonbird. "You have grown much too mature and dense for me to ever carry again."

"What do you mean?"

"I can only carry your airy, childlike spirit body now. The solid adult form of appetites, anger, and desires must be cut off, to stay behind in the world of real and heavy things."

"You mean I'll just *stay* there, mumbling and nodding? My physical form always waited for me while we did the healings—but this time I feel *afraid.*"

"Don't worry about your husk," said the Moonbird. "It will soon be discovered by some villagers guiding tourists on a mountain trek. They'll recognize you at once, and all the island will worship your physical body with reverence. They'll make pilgrimages to the volcano to pray to you. They'll feed and massage you, and build a small temple to house and protect you. They'll hang garlands around your neck, chant pujas and arrange offerings. Your dense physical body will be quite safe and content here while we fly together as phantasms in the flowing realm of illusions."

"After we heal Lasmi, I'll return to claim my body as usual," nodded Madai.

"*No.* You must choose," said the Moonbird. "If you want to live and feel as an ordinary man, I'll return you to the solid earth. If you want to heal Lasmi, you must fly away with me now. You can live as man or god. Not *both.*"

"You mean I must remain as a *ghost!*" cried Madai.

"If you wish to save Lasmi . . . You will be tenderly cared for by the islanders, who regard your body as a sacred treasure. You'll be fed coco-milk and massaged with oil. No harm will come to your flesh—and do you need it so badly? You felt no desire for food or drink, sleep or touch, or even breath when we flew under the sea. Do you miss those things so much?"

"I'll miss being touched," said Madai wistfully.

There was a swirl of white and blue and tangled copper, and the shard of Rangda appeared. She hovered large and angry before them, with one blazing, furious eye and a tusked, twisted mouth. "I dislike what I *see!*" hissed Rangda.

"Get away, witch!" shouted Madai.

"This time you must listen to *me*, my foolish son. That stupid sparrow has always envied your lifespark, and tried incessantly to deny you its joys. Isn't that so?"

"Perhaps," said Madai.

"That verminous bird once had his own flesh, as a rufous-eyed, ruthless eagle. He discarded himself to soar as a servant of Visnu, as an immortal and insignificant spirit. Now he wants to steal you because he still secretly envies your physical form. He wants to absorb and consume it. His own died long since and was eaten by worms—and he can't restore his flesh. Don't toss aside your*self* so blithesomely. Once it's destroyed—it's *gone*. That lice-eaten sparrow assures you of solicitous care, but how can you be so sure? Do simple villagers understand how to nurse an immobilized body in an inaccessible spot? To them it's a temple statue, to be polished sometimes and presented with offerings—then left to sit and rust. You suppose you'll be ministered to so well? Then *see* . . ."

Madai saw himself still sitting on the desolate rim of the volcano, mumbling and nodding as a steady, cold rain beat down. A small procession of awed villagers climbed up to the site, playing flutes and drums and singing melodious temple songs.

They arranged mango and lychee offerings at his feet, and hung garlands of fragrant frangipani around his neck. They gently spooned coco-milk into his mouth, and massaged his limbs with oil. They erected a small palm-frond pagoda over his head, which they decked with ornately painted images and elaborate towers of fruit and blossoms. They chanted to Madai and begged him to heal their ills. Then still singing, and playing their haunting flutes and rhythmic drums, they trekked back down the slopes of Mount Alāka.

Now Madai was all alone in this remote spot. The palm-frond shelter didn't prevent the cold rain from dripping down his skin. He sat entranced, mumbling and dozing. The garlands grew brown and wilted around his neck. The fruit offerings at his feet began to rot. Swarms of spiteful gnats bit his damp, festering skin. The rain stopped and intense sunlight burned his eyes. His flesh withered and his malnourished muscles atrophied. Spiders built patterned webs in his ears, and across his folded, immobile limbs. He exuded a sweet, musty odor.

Villagers and relatives still made the long and difficult trek to visit his living shrine—occasionally, when they were desperate to pray for good health. But as the novelty lessened, their visits were increasingly rare, for it was a tiring journey up the flank of the volcano.

When they came, they chanted melodiously, and brought the ritual offerings of flowers and fruit, coco-milk and sweet oil. They fed and massaged him, and repaired the palm-frond pagoda. But their visits were infrequent—and his body grew more and more neglected.

An expedition of American doctors and scientists, sponsored by Jana Davids and led by the New Zealander, Paul Robbes, climbed the volcano to observe Madai. They unanimously diagnosed a severe catatonic breakdown caused by extreme stress. They offered to take him to America for treatment, at Jana's expense, but the islanders refused to relinquish the sacred relic of his body.

Eventually his organs failed, and he evolved into a silent, mummified icon.

"See what happens to deserted bodies," hissed Rangda. "*See* . . . Rush back to yourself at once! Why sacrifice yourself for a silly girl? There are so many sweet girls for you to see . . ."

"If you return to your flesh, Lasmi will die," warned the Moonbird.

Madai looked anxiously from one spirit to the other. Which one was right? What should he do? Their faces began to whirl around him. The shimmering Moonbird and the flickering shard of Rangda . . . The shining Garuda and the raging Antagonist . . . Revolving and spinning around him so rapidly—that finally he couldn't tell them apart! Which was the Moonbird? Which was Rangda? Whirling . . . Revolving . . . Spinning in a glimmering and hissing blur.

Madai was trapped between two powerful and remorseless beings. It had all seemed so simple when he started his journey. He would find the Moonbird and heal Lasmi—nothing more. Now he must sacrifice himself to save her, and would lose her no matter what he chose. What should he *do?*

"You must decide quickly," said the Moonbird. "There's little time left. Her heart is growing weak, and Yama, black Lord of Death, is eager to claim her."

"This isn't necessary, my son," hissed the shard of Rangda, assuming the form of a lithe and lovely young woman with soft black eyes.

"Why destroy yourself to save one foolish wench? There are so many girls to see. This selfish sparrow wants to steal your spirit—hasten back inside your flesh! You'll live in the desa so peacefully. The villagers will worship you as a saint and they'll respect you now. You can live in pleasure and ease. *See* . . ."

Before Madai's eyes rose a vision of life in the desa, back inside his body—after the death of Lasmi. He had his own shrine and sleeping house in the family compound, and was called the Widowed Wise Man, and treated with deference and awe. Villagers came to him and politely asked for advice on intimate matters. They brought him fruit, fish, and rice, which his mother and the serving girls prepared in spicy curries.

Two lovely young women with soft black eyes served him and tended to his needs. They sang sweetly and danced for him. They cooked and cared for his garden. They washed and massaged him. He had few cares and responsibilities, and his flesh grew plump and the lines of his face were relaxed. He lived a long life of comfort, and all the people on the island honored him as one who speaks with the gods.

"You must choose," said the Moonbird. "Between the death of Lasmi, and a brief life of pleasure for yourself. Or the span of an immortal, living only in the fluctuating shadow world of the mind. You'll fly with me as a spirit, living as long as anyone, anywhere needs Madai the Healer. Many men would welcome the chance to elude the final cold caress of Yama, bull-headed Lord of Death. But you can never live among ordinary people, or eat with them—or touch them as a man again. Now you must decide."

"I never wanted to be a god! I was *happy* as a normal man." Madai's eyes had the fearful look of a hunted animal.

The whirling stopped and Madai sat very quietly atop the Garuda, and thought. He could easily do as Rangda urged. Reclaim his body, pass himself off as a saint and wise man, and live a lazy life of ease, reading and advising others—for a few short years until entropy finally captured him.

He was growing older now. In just a fleeting handful of decades he must inevitably face the awful pain of aging, and wagering his life in the futile dice game with Yama, bull-headed Lord of Death. Then he'd become a lonely ghost, wandering like Dawan in her sad and beautiful garden. Perhaps he shouldn't cling so selfishly to his body. Dawan had said he'd lose it soon enough.

Should he fly with the Moonbird, living on eternally? He could live through Lasmi, and see the island through her eyes. Through Lasmi he could watch the ongoing shadow drama of desa life. If she found new happiness, he could learn to take pleasure in her joy. After Lasmi finished her span of years, and even after his own flesh died, he could live on with the Moonbird—as a phantasm. He would heal those who needed him and watch the world through the eyes of ordinary people—forever. This appealed to his innate boyish curiosity. He would always find out what happened next, and Madai's story would never end. He would cheat Yama, implacable Lord of Death, at his loaded dice game.

"We'll sail away from the churning confusion of the island and see a bright procession of wonders," whispered the Moonbird.

"Let's fly to Lasmi and get right to work," said Madai, with a rueful little smile. "Now that I've become a figment of my own imagination."

33

Lasmi's eyes, glittering darkly in her pale, sunken face, announced that she was still alive. Her battle continued, though she was nearly defeated by weakness and pain. Lasmi still survived inside those luminous eyes—but would not for very long.

Madai was shocked by her fragility and tears burned his own eyes. The wasting sickness had progressed quickly and she was nearly gone. Could they still save her, or had he abandoned his own body for naught?

"I must talk to her," he said.

"Her mind is open and receptive now. Try whispering in her ear," said the Moonbird, calm as a mountain peak or a sun-streaked sea.

They glided to her mat in the wicker sleeping house, and Madai jumped off the Moonbird and knelt down to her.

"Lasmi," he called quietly.

She turned her head very slowly and smiled slightly. She showed no surprise at the sound of his voice, but the brightening of those great black eyes showed her relief that he'd finally appeared.

"I'm so glad you're here, Madai," she whispered. "I'm dying. I can feel my strength seeping away like sweat. I move in and out of confused sleep, and each day it's harder to waken. I sink deeper into suffocating mists—and soon I'll never wake again. I'm frightened of dying—can you help me stay awake, Madai?"

"You'll feel better soon," he said. "I've brought the Moonbird to help you. Whatever happens, remember that I'll be with you—always."

Lasmi nodded and her eyes grew more peaceful.

Madai felt saddened as he explored the caverns of her body. If it had been anyone else, he would have announced that the disease had progressed too far to be cured, but this was his beloved Lasmi. He'd made his decision and his promise. He would heal her. Somehow.

Inside the honeycombed labyrinth of bone marrow, the blood

cells divide and take form. Inside her leukemia-ridden bones, the process had gone berserk. Instead of the healthy flotilla of fat, red, doughnut-shaped cells, bursting with nourishing oxygen, Madai saw limp, deflated cells of pale, sickly pink. Instead of aggressive ivory-colored spheres, he saw a straggle of deformed and wilted white cells.

All the normal blood corpuscles were crowded and weakened by a profusion of fat, grayish blobs that secreted a toxic slime. They resembled featureless slugs. These slug-shaped leukemia cells divided wildly inside her bone marrow and replaced the wholesome blood.

The grayish slugs traveled from her bones to the tubular blood vessels that fed her flesh. Instead of the hearty procession of red and white cells, there was a struggling straggle of corpuscles, crowded by an aggressive surge of slimy slugs. The fat gray blobs circulated to every organ of her body. Instead of nourishing her with vital oxygen, they fastened onto her cell walls like leeches, exuding toxic slime, which slowly ate into the healthy tissues.

They seemed especially drawn to her nerves. The neatly bundled strands and folds of neural cells still flashed and pulsed with surges of electrochemical energy, but the bundles were festooned with clusters of the toxic leeches that clung greedily to the neural sheaths. Lasmi's nervous system looked like a dying shrub that was infested with a horrid, clinging parasite. Soon she would perish from lack of oxygen and the noxious poisons. Very soon.

"What can we *do?*" asked Madai. "There are so many of them. They're all over and new ones form constantly!"

"What do you do when a valuable fruit tree is infected with caterpillars?" asked the Moonbird.

"We buy spray from the Chinese store. If we can't afford spray, then the children crush the worms by hand, one by one. But that would take forever!"

"Do you have other plans?" asked the Moonbird. "You're no longer bound by mortal time."

"I suppose that's true. I have nothing else to do now. Let's begin in her brain, where they can do the quickest damage."

In Lasmi's brain, the flashing neural bundles were folded into orderly, convoluted patterns—contaminated by clinging clusters of poisonous gray leeches. Shifting patterns of light inside her mind revealed her thoughts. Madai saw brief flashes of her girlhood in the desa. He saw her intently reading an old *National Geographic* at the mission school, and happily bathing at the lotus pond with Dawan.

He saw carefree days gathering passion fruit in the forest, and quiet afternoons cooking a scanty meal with her mother and younger sister in their shabby compound. He saw her eluding the hungry gaze of widower Ram, and he saw sweet, sad, intimate images of their own marriage. But it was all dominated by the feeble misery of a mind that was slowly suffocating in the intrusive growth of ugly, abnormal cells.

He felt waves of anger mixed with revulsion. He would kill the wretched things—all of them! He began to mash them with his hands until their stinging slime ran down his arms. They popped easily, like soggy bubbles. They didn't try to escape or offer any resistance, unlike the germbugs. But there were so many of them, and new ones poured in constantly through her bloodstream. As soon as a cluster of leeches was cleaned away, new growths formed.

"What can we do?" asked Madai, with despair in his eyes. "They're everywhere! They'll eat into a vital organ soon, and she'll die while we're frantically popping them, one by one. Are we already too late? We *must* think of a better way to kill them—I need a great flock of Moonbirds to gobble them up, like sea gulls gobble schools of tiny fish."

"Close your eyes," said the Garuda.

"Why?"

"Close them and be quiet for a moment—this requires all my attention."

Madai obediently shut his eyes, and suddenly he felt a wrenching sensation and a tremendous explosion of brilliant, colorless light. Had Lasmi suffered a stroke? He tried to open his eyes, but the light was blinding.

"Shut them!" barked the Moonbird in a strangely echoing voice.

There was another wrench and another explosion of light. Then another and another in staccato bursts like machine-gun fire. Madai felt elating surges of strength. His powers were boundless—as a god's. Then it was quiet and dark.

"Open your eyes," commanded the Moonbird.

He opened his eyes and saw that there was no longer one frail Madai seated atop one glowing Moonbird. Instead there were thousands of shimmering Garudas holding thousands of glistening Madais—no longer made of flesh, but of the same shining substance as the Moonbird.

"What happened?" asked the myriad moonstone Madais in surprised echoes.

"We're no longer limited to material boundaries," replied the swarms of glimmering Moonbirds, voices aloof and passionless as the sound of crystals ringing and resounding.

The many prismatic Madais watched each other, perched atop the countless glowing Moonbirds. They fanned through Lasmi's body like a shower of blazing sparks, crushing the slimy gray leeches that clung to her nerves, blood vessels, and flesh. The noxious slug-cells divided and reproduced endlessly, and traveled through her bloodstream to fasten greedily upon her tissues. But the multiple gleaming warriors waited at each cobbled blood vessel and organ to crush them.

Gradually they made headway, and the images that flashed inside her mind slowly shifted from pain and suffering to strength and relief. Time coiled into itself as they battled in the endless twilight, moving through Lasmi to destroy the deadly gray cells.

Her mind flashes showed that she was feeling much better. She sat up and ate a little rice gruel, then walked slowly around the courtyard, leaning on Bapak's arm. She rested in the shade of an orchid-twined mango tree, and combed her tangled black hair carefully. She waited with a small smile for Madai, her lover and healer, to return to the desa and rejoice with her.

The Madais who fought so tirelessly realized sadly that she didn't know he no longer existed as a man. He had become a sparkling phantasm who could never return to her—or embrace her again.

Lasmi sat smiling in the shade of the mango tree, her long hair prettily combed. She felt much better, and she hummed a temple song as she waited for Madai to appear. Time passed and the sun arced overhead. She felt stronger and stronger—but Madai never came. The smile faded and she grew tired and wistful. Where *was* Madai? He must have journeyed very far away. The pain and poisonous suffocation were lifting—but was *he* hurt in the forest? She wanted to stroke his warm cheek, and thank him for finding the Moonbird to heal her. Lasmi felt tired and fretful and sad. Her strength was just returning and she needed to rest. Finally she went to her sleeping mat, forgetting all about her hair, and drifted into a restless sleep.

The battling Madais watched the pictures in her mind with lonely melancholy, and a longing to leap back inside his body to embrace and console her. But Madai's physical form had been abandoned, entranced, on the desolate rim of the volcano.

There was a lull. Lasmi drifted into a more peaceful sleep, and only vague, shifting patterns of light and random images formed in her mind. The clinging clusters of noxious gray slugs, and the lethal matrix in the bone marrow where they formed, had been destroyed. Lasmi would feel well again, and live her natural span.

Madai and Lasmi would miss and mourn each other always, but he felt content, knowing she would survive.

"Close your eyes," commanded the myriad Moonbirds in echoing voices.

The countless Madais closed their eyes, and felt a wild spinning. When he opened them, he and the Garuda had reformed into single entities again. There was only one Moonbird and only one Madai—but no longer a man of flesh. He was now an immortal being of shining moonstone.

Having given up one kind of love, he had gained a greater self. No longer immersed in pain, joy, sorrow, he felt the surge of the tides and the flow of light from the sun and stars. Soaring high above his native island, he saw . . . heard . . . felt . . . the rivers flow into the sea.

And he observed that the sea was never filled.

Madai and the Moonbird hovered in a realm of cobalt blue beyond the sky. "We can rest now," said the Moonbird.

"How can we rest without real bodies?" asked Madai.

"Our bodies are real in their own way. We have no need for sleep, but we can relax. Where shall we go now?"

"Where *can* we go?"

"Almost anywhere—except back to our physical forms."

"I should heal the other villagers. I promised not to forget them—but first I want to fly to the moon. Now that I'm an immortal, I can *walk* on the moon with my own bare feet, and sip the invigorating moon-milk. Is that possible?"

"Most things are possible."

"We'll make footprints on the moon, like spacemen, and strengthen ourselves with moon-milk, then we'll return to the island to heal the villagers."

"Then we can rest," said the Moonbird.

"No. We'll dive beneath the opal sea to the Naga Queen's palace."

"Very good," said the Moonbird. "We can linger in the exquisite underwater city of *Bhogavati*, built of gold and coral and pearls, where cobra-hooded Mahanagini and her elegant court reside. They play strange and wonderful music, blowing delicate conch shells, and they perform endless shadow dances. Many spirits and sea dragons dwell in the filigreed palace, enjoying the timeless performance. They will gladly welcome you to their aquatic realm. We can pass many eons there, now that you're no longer tied to linear time."

"But I would soon grow bored with interminable puppet plays. My monkey mind is too restless, as my friend Hanuman would say."

"*So?*" the Garuda asked dryly.

"So I want to heal the blind Naga prince. We must restore his sight and his growth, and raise an army of monkeys and loyalist Naga-dragon soldiers. We'll march with Queen Mahanagini and the Naga prince, grown bright-eyed and strong, to regain his father's, Basudara's, throne, which was stolen by the rebels at the cremation ceremony."

"*Then* can we rest?" asked the Moonbird. "My wings brush the sun and stars, and my eyes see above and below the earth. There are so many wonders in the infinite vastness of my floating realm. We have spacious expanses of time to enjoy them all."

"I want to see all your phantasms—but first I must do one more thing," said Madai.

"What's that?" asked the Moonbird wearily.

"I'll appear to Lasmi—just as you appeared to me long ago. She heard me clearly when I whispered in her ear, and her mind is very keen. I think she can hear beyond ordinary sound, and perhaps she can learn to see beyond ordinary sight. I must speak to her again—and show her my new form. Maybe someday she'll fly with us as a crystalline immortal."

"You want me to carry *both* of you?" sighed the Moonbird.

"Figments can do almost anything," smiled Madai as they rose upward to the moon.

On the island they say that from time to time the flickering blue lights of the evil lantern ship appear beyond the reef, to lure the fishermen to their deaths in their flimsy, fish-headed boats. But whenever the terrible ship appears, two great shooting stars dance across the sky to drive it away before it can cause any harm. The villagers say that those blazing lights are Madai and the Moonbird, still guarding the island.

The tale is ended, but the story goes on forever . . .